DEEP TERROR

ERIC S BROWN

SEVERED PRESS
HOBART TASMANIA

DEEP TERROR

Copyright © 2022 Eric S Brown

WWW.SEVEREDPRESS.COM

ISBN: 978-1-922551-39-9

DEEP TERROR

Being nervous was an odd experience for Marshal Robert McShane and not one that he cared for. The world had changed so much in the past few years. The introduction of "Everlasting" only further served to separate the lower and middle classes in America from the upper class. The revitalizing drug offered a longer life to those who could afford it, increasing the average lifespan by a minimum of twenty years while mega corporations and governments vied for power. And there was only one place on Earth where the genetic material needed to produce Everlasting could be harvested – the Pioneer 4 station.

Pioneer 4 was located at the bottom of the Atlantic Ocean next to an oceanic trench, codenamed Deep Black. The station's crew was a mix of civilian scientists, engineers, sub pilots, and a military contingent assigned there to protect it. In total, after he and the other new arrivals reached the station, there would be twenty-five souls living within its heavily armored walls. The population was equally divided with McShane being the odd man out, answering neither to the military commanding officer or Pioneer 4's chief scientist. His job was to keep the peace between the two groups, ensuring the source material for Everlasting continued to flow to the surface world above.

The rear compartment of the sub was cramped despite the fact that only four of its six seats contained occupants. The area was small with tight, closed in, metal walls that gave it a very claustrophobic atmosphere. McShane sat in the forward seat near the doorway that led into the pilot compartment. Stealing a glance over his shoulder, he looked at the others again - Dr. Angela Lowery, Privates Steward and Duffman, and Wrinkler, who was the epitome of everything nerdy. McShane had read all their files. He knew Wrinkler was an engineering tech though according to his file the young man held numerous degrees in several fields with an IQ that was off the charts. Only Wrinkler seemed to be excited to be headed down to the station on the ocean floor. The two privates were stone faced and looked as nervous as McShane was himself. Dr. Lowery had her laptop open and was studying something on its screen intently, living up to what her file said about the woman being a workaholic.

Something akin to a shudder ran through the walls of the compartment causing them to vibrate and McShane to flinch. Wrinkler must have noticed because the young man leaned forward in his seat and said, "Don't worry, sir. These subs are built to withstand the pressure down here. I've never heard of one of them rupturing."

McShane grunted in response to the tech's words. In his mind he was picturing the exterior of the sub surrounded by the darkness of the depths they were in. The sub didn't look anything like what one would think. Its design and appearance were much more like that of some kind of orbital dropship from a science fiction movie, somewhere between a square and rectangular shape, thickly armored, and bulky rather than sleek.

Wrinkler flopped back into his seat, frowning, but McShane didn't give a crap. He had no desire to strike up a conversation with the tech. There would be plenty of time for everyone to get to know one another on Pioneer 4. Though shipments of the source material for Everlasting were shot upwards to the surface every day, manned trips only happened once every few months and all of them had signed up for a full year of employment inside the walls of Pioneer 4.

Clicking loose the safety harness of his seat, McShane rose and headed for the pilot compartment. His status as Pioneer 4's new marshal gave him the power to enter it with nothing more than a wave of his badge at the door's sensor. The pilots looked up from the sub's controls with surprised expressions.

"Marshal?" Lieutenant Winston asked. "Is there something we can help you with?"

McShane shook his head. "Just wanted to take a gander at Pioneer 4 before we dock with it."

The window in the pilot compartment wasn't overly large and he knew it was strengthened against more than just the pressure of the depths. None the less, the lieutenant motioned for him to come closer to it. McShane rested a hand on the back of Winston's seat, and peered out the window. Amid the darkness, far below, the station's exterior lights lit it up. There were more lights around it marking the station's defensive perimeter and still others which illuminated a pathway to where the gaping oceanic trench McShane heard about had to be located. The whole place was much larger than he'd imagined it to be. Pioneer 4 itself was an ugly thing which rested upon an X-shaped foundation of supports that were designed to stabilize the station in the event of seismic activity. Around the station and the path leading to the trench was a continuous metal fence braced by thick titanium poles. Every couple of seconds a crackle of deadly energy ran along its length. The only movement to be seen were the hulking forms of two mecha lumbering out of the station, presumably on their way to the trench.

"Looks pretty dead around the place right now," Lieutenant Winston told him, "But trust me, it's not like this most of the time."

McShane gave him a questioning look.

The lieutenant shrugged. "I'm sure you were briefed on everything down here, sir. Doubt there's anything I could tell you that you don't already know about. Anyway, sir, if you don't mind, it would be best if you returned to your seat as we're about to start our approach."

He really didn't want to but McShane nodded politely at the lieutenant and did as he was asked. The others in the rear compartment were all watching him as he entered it again. McShane figured they were wondering why he'd gone in the forward compartment and if there was trouble they needed to know about.

"Everything okay?" Dr. Lowery ventured cautiously. He could hear the concern in her voice.

"Just getting in some sightseeing before we dock with the station," McShane said. "Everything's fine out there."

The two privates sitting behind Dr. Lowery and Wrinkler visibly relaxed. The two of them had been tensed up, wearing tense expressions. They knew much better than the civilians exactly what the sub could run into on its way to the station.

****

The two Silt Stompers marched along the path towards the "Deep Black". Pioneer 4's sensors were picking up some activity in the trench and Captain Wrightman wasn't in the mood to take any risks. Riggs and Noah had been dispatched to put an end to any trouble before things ever got the chance to get dicey. The captain hadn't been the same since the crap that had gone down inside the station that cost the lives of five of its personnel, including Dr. Milner and Marshal Hershey. In truth, Riggs doubted that anyone had really. He sure as hell hadn't himself. After all that mess, there was a profound lack of trust for each other among all of Pioneer 4's crew. Dr. Foxx was doing all she could for everyone, trying to boost morale and requiring them all to attend a minimum of at least one weekly therapy session with her. If those mandated sessions were doing anything other than offering material for some good jokes or ticking a few more stubborn crew members off, Riggs couldn't see it.

"Hey," Noah's voice rang out through the comm. in his suit's helmet. "Check that out!"

The head of Riggs' Silt Stomper swiveled round just enough for him to see that the right arm of Noah's mecha was extended upwards. Looking in the direction it was pointing, Riggs saw the lights of a drop sub coming down towards Pioneer 4.

"I bet that's the new marshal coming in,"

Noah told him.

"Yeah," Riggs responded. "I think I remember the captain saying that was happening today."

"It's about time," Noah sighed. "Maybe this guy can really get things back together down here."

"Let's hope so," Riggs said and glanced at the upper right quadrant of his Silt Stomper's tactical display. "But right now, we need to focus, man. We got a job to get done."

"Right," Noah assured him. "Don't you fret none, Sarge. We got this. We got this by the arse."

Riggs chuckled despite himself, bringing the weapon systems of his Silt Stomper online.

Each of the Silt Stompers stood twelve feet tall. They were state of the art machines of walking destruction, built to withstand the pressure of the depths and lay waste to anything they encountered within them. Their name came from the amount of silt they stirred up as they walked across the ocean floor. Riggs didn't know who came up with the name but it certainly fit the heavy mechs.

A Silt Stomper was more armored than an Abrams tank and built for full out war. Each Silt Stomper carried an array of weapons, ranging from shoulder mounted needle guns to arm mounted, mini torpedo launchers. They were the best and most powerful underwater killing machines that money could buy. In addition to their armor and weapons, Silt Stompers were equipped with high grade optics allowing for clarity of vision in the worst conditions and advanced sonar units as well. Nothing was ever going to be able to sneak up on them under the water without detonating an EMP first.

The Silt Stompers were built solely to protect the Pioneer stations after the first three had been utterly wiped out by the creatures that lived in the Deep Black. And the designs of each Pioneer station had been upgraded after each loss, too. Pioneer 4 was a fortress that nothing from the Deep Black was ever likely to be able to breach as they had its predecessors. Hell, Riggs thought, Pioneer 4 had more than just its armor and the Silt Stompers; this version of the station even had a continually energy shielded hull that was capable of frying anything that made contact with it.

The two mechs stopped several dozen yards back from the edge of the Deep Black. Riggs cranked his Silt Stomper's sensors to full power, targeting the darkness within the trench.

"You seeing what I'm seeing?" Noah's voice asked over his comm.

Riggs was. Over a hundred of the creatures that lived in the trench were amassing just beneath the lip of it that the Silt Stompers were facing. Something had riled the monsters up. Riggs figured it was the descent of the transport sub bringing down the new marshal and replacement crew. The sub was well behind them and safe, already likely in the process of docking with Pioneer 4. They didn't need to worry about it straying into their line of fire.

"When they come out, it's going to be hard and fast," Riggs warned.

"Think we should dig in?" Noah's voice was calm. They had both been up against this many of the monsters and more before.

Riggs nodded though he knew Noah couldn't see him as he answered, "Yeah. I think so, just in case they manage to get close and swarm us."

The Silt Stompers were equipped with diamond tipped anchor drills that now emerged from their feet, tearing downward into the silt and rock below it to lock into place. Riggs saw on his tactical display that the mech's bracing anchors lights were green, not that he planned on letting any of the monsters reach him.

"Should we give them a little reminder of human firepower?" Noah chuckled, the left arm of his Stomper showing off its torpedo launcher towards Riggs.

"Nah," Riggs said. "Let's save the ordnance. We'll hit them as they come out. Shoulder guns on my mark."

"Copy that," Noah assured him.

Watching the edge of the Deep Black, Riggs

shuddered inside his Silt Stomper. As many times as he'd done this, the things living in the trench never failed to creep him out. They were a hideous mixture of humanity and a toothy Anglerfish. Their arms were overly long like those of a primate and instead of skin, their bodies were covered in midnight black, armored scales. Razor sharp, talon-like nails tipped the ends of their fingers. The things were fragging strong too, far stronger than a man. The only thing good about them was that they were, most of the time anyway, dumb as rocks. If one of them fell, wounded, the others would swarm it in a feeding frenzy, tearing it apart. Riggs shook his head to clear it in an attempt to get his focus back to where it needed to be. The monsters were coming.

Feral, yellow eyes glowed with rage beneath the ridges of bone above them on the faces of the monsters as they came swarming out of the Deep Black. Their teeth gleamed in the beams of light the Silt Stompers directed at the creatures.

"Open fire!" Riggs barked, activating his mech's shoulder guns. The tribarrels of the weapons spun, hosing the emerging fish men with streams of high velocity dart-like needles.

Noah's mech opened up on the creatures too. The first wave of the fish men were ripped apart by the rounds pouring into them. The water near the trench grew black with their putrid blood. The Silt Stompers didn't let up though. Their shoulder guns continued to hammer the ranks of the swarming fish men.

"The fragging things are too dumb to know when they're beaten," Noah laughed.

"Don't get cocky," Riggs cautioned the younger mech pilot. "This ain't over yet."

Despite the combined fire of the two mecha, some of the fish men were managing to make it through their barrage. . . or rather around it. A handful of the creatures had darted to the far left, right, or shot upwards. The Silt Stompers' guns couldn't adjust to the moving targets fast enough to get them all, given the number of the creatures. Riggs wasn't worried about it. . . yet. As long as the monsters remained focused on them, there wouldn't be a problem. Pioneer 4 was safe regardless. It would take more than a few of the things to threaten the station. What did give him slight cause for concern was the sub that was still in docking maneuvers. If the creatures went after it, the sub might be damaged before they could stop it from happening.

"Sarge," Noah said, as if reading his thoughts.

"Hold your position, Noah, and stay anchored," Riggs ordered.

His gamble paid off as one of the fish men came screeching towards his Silt Stomper from its right flank. The creature slammed itself into the armor of the mech, claws raking over the suit's armor, attempting to rend it as if the metal were flesh. The overly bold fish thing paid for that mistake as its talon-like nails broke. Careful not to reach into his own line of fire with the hand of his Silt Stomper, Riggs grabbed the fish man, steel fingers closing around its neck. The pressure of the mech's grip popped the thing's head from its shoulders in an explosion of foul, black, ink-like blood.

The other creatures who had escaped from the onslaught of the two Silt Stompers came at them too. As he saw they were fully committed to the melee, Riggs shouted, "Disengage anchors and let's tear these mothers up."

"Yes sir!" Noah shouted, battle induced excitement filling his voice.

The shoulder guns of the Silt Stompers stopped firing, their barrels slowing to a rest, as Riggs and Noah took their own approaches to finishing the few remaining creatures.

A gleaming sword blade sprung out of his Silt Stomper's right forearm as its anchors retracted from the ocean floor. A fish man hurled itself straight into the front of Riggs' suit, the thing's yellow eyes peering in at him through the mecha's eye slits. Riggs jerked up his Silt Stomper's blade in between the fish man's legs. It continued upwards through the creature's body, cleaving the thing in half as easily as if it were slicing butter. Riggs spun his Silt Stomper about, grabbing another of the creatures by its leg. The limb was tugged free from the thing's body in a burst of black blood. Riggs hadn't intended to tear the leg off. He'd intended to swing the creature around into another that was barreling towards him. The fast-moving fish man thudded into the front of his Silt Stomper. The impact rocked the heavy mech but even with its anchors up it wasn't enough to knock the Silt Stomper over. Riggs swung at the creature with the mech's extended sword. It slashed through the fish man at an angle, cutting clean through armored scales and bone alike.

Noah was taking a much more hands on approach with his efforts to end the last of the fish men that had come after him. His Silt Stomper punched its metal fists through one creature after another. Razor talons slashed vainly against the Silt Stomper's armor, unable to breach it. Noah caught hold of a fish, slamming the madly thrashing creature into the ocean floor. As he released it, the fish man floated upwards, face bashed into oozing, black pulp from the impact. Noah had already moved on, charging his Silt Stomper in between two more of the creatures. The mech's left hand lashed out, punching through the chest of the creature on that side of it. The Silt Stomper's fist emerged from the creature's back, a section of spinal chord clutched within it, the fish man dying instantly. Meanwhile, the right hand of his mech snapped out to take hold of the other creature's skull, metal fingers sinking into it. The fish man's body jerked and twitched about beneath the Silt Stomper's hold on its head.

There was only one of the creatures left alive. It had streaked passed them while they were finishing up the others. The sensors of Riggs' Silt Stomper warned him of it as the creature sped towards the sub settling in place at Pioneer 4's docking port. There was no way his mech could intercept it. Silt Stompers just couldn't match the speed of the creatures from the Deep Black. They weren't built for it.

"Noah!" Riggs shouted over the comm. "One got through!"

"Roger that," Noah responded. "I'm on it."

Unlike Riggs, Noah's Silt Stomper was already facing towards Pioneer 4 and didn't have to waste precious seconds adjusting its position. The young pilot activated the auto targeting system, not willing to risk making such a long distance shot himself in the direction of the sub. It took over for him as his Silt Stomper's right side, shoulder mounted needle gun raised upwards, taking aim at the creature. The weapon fired a single burst of needles that caught up to the fish man, plunging into the back of its skull and emerging through the center of his forehead in a burst of black blood, small fragments of shattered bone, and brain matter.

"Nice shot," Riggs teased Noah, knowing the younger pilot hadn't made it himself.

"Thanks," Noah answered anyway.

Riggs swept the area around them and the edge of the Deep Black with his sensors on their max. setting. Everything was clear.

"Looks like we got them all," Riggs said.

"Like there was ever any doubt that we would," Noah snorted.

"Come on, kid," Riggs sighed. "Let's head back."

****

Marshsal Robert McShane stood next to Dr. Lowery and the others inside the connecting airlock between the docked sub and Pioneer 4. The pilots of the sub had been listening to the comm. Chatter between the Silt Stompers who were out there engaging creatures that emerged from the trench known as the Deep Black. Apparently, any danger to the sub was over and the two mechs were now returning to the station. He noticed Dr. Lowery stealing glances at him as they waited for the airlock leading into Pioneer 4 to open.

"Were we in danger out there?" Dr. Lowery finally broke down and asked.

McShane shook his head. "No, ma'am. I was briefed on the details of this place before getting on the sub that brought us down. The things that came out of that trench never had a prayer of reaching us with two Silt Stompers out there."

Dr. Lowery didn't look as if she really believed him but McShane didn't care. He had told her the truth. Her bright green eyes locked with his for a fraction of a second before both of them turned their heads towards the airlock as it dilated open to admit them. McShane felt something stir within him that he hadn't in a very long, long time in that fleeting moment.

Colonel Ashley Hendricks stood with two of her troops, waiting for them, in the corridor beyond the airlock. McShane could see her looking them all over, giving them a quick appraisal before speaking.

"Welcome to Pioneer 4," Colonel Hendricks greeted them as they stepped out of the airlock into the station. Her hands were clasped behind her back and the colonel kept them there as if standing at attention. With nothing more than a nod indicating they should move along, she dismissed Privates Steward and Duffman, leaving only the engineering tech standing with McShane and Dr. Lowery.

"Where's Dr. Jeffery?" Dr. Lowery asked, clearly surprised he wasn't there to greet them with the colonel.

With a snort of contempt, Colonel Hendricks answered, "He's in his lab, of course. The good doctor seldom leaves it these days. My man here, Gunther, will take you to him."

"If you'll follow me, Doc," the hulking giant of a man that stood with the colonel said.

"Guess I'll catch you later," Dr. Lowery flashed McShane a wry grin.

"I imagine so," McShane answered.

As Gunther led Dr. Lowery away down a side corridor, Colonel Hendricks kept her eyes on him. McShane wasn't a telepath but didn't need to be one to know what was likely going through her head. He couldn't blame the colonel. The previous Marshal, Aldis Hershey, had gone insane, killing four of Pioneer 4's crew before she'd been able to stop him. The reports McShane read were sketchy as to the details of why Hershey had done what he did but that had no effect upon the horror, shock, and loss those serving down here on Pioneer 4 had endured because of those actions.

"I imagine you'd like to be brought up to speed on the conditions here," Colonel Hendricks commented.

"That would be a good place to start," McShane agreed.

"Allow me to take you to your office," she said. "It would be better for us to talk there."

McShane cocked an eyebrow at her, wondering what the colonel had meant by the last bit. The reports had mentioned that tensions were running hot between the military and civilian contingents of the crew but even so.

. .The colonel not wanting to speak openly sent up all the wrong kind of signals. If things were that bad, it was hard to understand why the colonel hadn't just declared martial law in order to simply deal with the civilians as she saw fit. He certainly would have done so in her place.

"What's up with your guard?" McShane glanced at the solider who had remained with the colonel.

"Chief Beckett," Colonel Hendricks said, indicating that the chief should be the one to answer.

"I'm not a guard, sir. I'm here to help address any questions you might have about Pioneer 4, sir," Beckett explained. "As the head engineer of the military contingent, Colonel Hendricks thought my presence might be useful."

"I thought the civilian engineer that just came down with me was going to be over all engineering issues that arise inside this station?" Marshal McShane challenged the chief.

"That is true, sir," Beckett nodded. "However. . ."

"However," Colonel Hendricks cut in, "the chief is more than capable of giving you a second opinion on any issues that do come up should you need it. In addition, he can address any concerns you might have about the Silt Stomper Mecha."

"And should I have concerns about them?" Marshal McShane frowned.

"We are beginning to run low on some types of ordanance, Marshal," the chief was frowning as well. "We're still well within the standard safety protocols for what we should have in storage but. . ."

"But the creatures from the Deep Black, their attacks on the stations are increasing in frequency," Marshal McShane finished for him.

"How did you. . ." Chief Beckett's eyes had gone wide.

"The reports that the brass upstairs gave me mentioned it," Marshal McShane explained with a slight shrug. "They didn't seem overly concerned about the situation with the creatures either."

"Nor should they be," Colonel Hendricks smiled. "My men and I are more than capable of keeping those things under control and this base safe."

Marshal McShane felt the urge to point out that she and her people had failed to stop the previous Marshal's killing spree. Instead, he said, "Sadly, Chief, as your C.O. there knows, there's not a lot I can do about supply issues but if you'll make a list of what you need, I'll include it in my first official report about this station and its status."

"Thank you, Marshal," Chief Beckett beamed.

The trio reached their destination. McShane hadn't paid much attention to the corridors they'd passed through on the way. All of them were gloomy and looked much the same to him. Besides, he'd studied the layout of the base already and trusted that he would be able to find his way about easily enough.

Chief Beckett opened the door of his office for him. The room behind it was more spacious than Marshal McShane thought it would be. There was a desk in its center and several cabinets surrounding it. There was a full out, CIC level, security monitoring station near the deck and an impressive eight screens on the wall in front of it. McShane noticed that there were still framed pictures of Marshal Hershey and his family on the deck and mounted on the walls across from the security monitoring screens. He moved to pick one of them up from the deck. In the picture, Hershey was holding a dark haired woman, presumably his wife, tightly about the waist as two children, a boy and girl, played in the open space of green grass covered lawn behind them.

"My apologies, Marshal McShane," Colonel Hendricks said. "I assumed the civilian crew had already prepared the office for you."

"And your people had more important things to attend to," McShane commented, being careful not to make the statement sound like an accusation. "Doesn't matter. I am actually glad

Hershey's stuff is still here. Looking at this picture, he sure doesn't seem like someone who would kill anyone who didn't deserve it. The reports I was given say that Hershey went insane."

"He was crazy at the end, alright," Chief Beckett nodded. "No doubt about that."

Marshal McShane ignored Beckett, staring at the colonel. "Before we get to that sitrep, Colonel, what can you tell me about what exactly happened down here that led to Hershey losing his crap?"

Colonel Hendricks took a moment as if choosing her words carefully before answering, "My best guess is that the strain got to him. The man was never comfortable living in this base and that didn't help matters."

"What strain?" Marshal McShane pressed.

Chief Beckett looked towards the colonel, seeking her permission before speaking up. She made no motion for him not to so Beckett said, "The science folks have been picking up some really odds things coming out of the Deep Black in the last couple of months. Dr. Miller was Dr. Jeffery's number two, Marshal. Miller claimed that some of these new "signals", as he called them, emerging from the Deep Black were more than just the ordinary energy pulses emitted from the trench."

"Were they?" Marshal McShane asked.

"That's a bit outside of my field, sir. I really

couldn't say," Chief Beckett shrugged.

"Dr. Jeffery has never confirmed Dr. Milner's claims," Colonel Hendricks added.

"And Marshal Hershey?" Marshal McShane walked around the desk to take a seat in what was now his chair.

"I won't lie or sugarcoat things for you, McShane," Colonel Hendricks huffed. "When Hershey first arrived, like I said, he was already struggling with living inside a structure whose walls could collapse and bring the ocean crashing down on him. The man just couldn't ever seem to get used to this environment. Hershey did his job well enough though and got on with most folks here."

"How does that tie in with Dr. Miller's claims?" Marshal McShane watched the colonel closely.

"When Dr. Jeffery wouldn't lend credence to what Miller had discovered, the good doctor approached Marshal Hershey with his wild theories of something in the Deep Black trying to make contact with us," Colonel Hendricks continued. "The Marshal became obsessed with them. Around that time, there were accidents in first the primary storage area and then in the Silt Stomper bay. No one died in either of those but there were folks injured in both. The civilians blamed my men for the screw up in storage and some among my people believe that it was someone among the civilians who sabotaged the ordinance that injured a mech pilot and one of my Silt Stomper techs."

"I see," Marshal McShane leaned forward, locking his hands together atop his desk. "I imagine no one knows for certain what happened in either of those incidents even now."

"You would be correct in that assumption too," Colonel Hendricks admitted. "I know no one under my command was responsible for the accident in storage. I can't say the same about the civilians and the Silt Stomper bay, though. It could have been bad luck or something much more sinister. There's just no means of knowing for sure."

"Marshal Hershey, what was his response to these accidents and accusations?" McShane's frown grew more intense.

"Not much," Colonel Hendricks answered. "He kept us from tearing each other apart, breaking up more than a few fights, but ultimately Hershey did nothing that broke the air of growing distrust and paranoia. Hershey retreated to his office for the most part, spending a great deal of time with Dr. Miller, only emerging if there was something truly dangerous happening within the station."

"Then one day, he just snapped," Chief Beckett chimed in.

"Marshal Hershey called a mandatory meeting for all of Pioneer 4's crew," Colonel

Hendricks was shaking her head. "It was there he went berserk. Shot two of my men before they even had a chance to react. Myself and others returned fire, forcing Hershey to flee. He made it to the Silt Stomper bay and took out my head engineer there before we could catch up to him. Cornered, with nowhere to run, we tried to reason with Hershey but the man was too far gone. He just kept rambling about something we hadn't seen yet living in the Deep Black until he finally opened fire on us again. At that point, we couldn't risk handling him with kid gloves anymore."

"You shot him dead in the Silt Stomper bay?" Marshal McShane said.

"We did," Colonel Hendricks looked directly at him. "There was no other choice, Marshal."

"It wasn't until later that we all discovered what Hershey had done to Dr. Milner," Chief Beckett added.

"Hershey had cut the poor bastard up." Colonel Hendricks' expression was one of utter disgust as she told him, "I'll freely admit that I despised Dr. Milner. The little bastard had always rubbed me the wrong way. Even so, no human being deserved to die like he did. You see, Marshal Hershey had tied Miller to a table in his own lab and dissected the doctor. I mean literally cut him up alive as if he were doing an autopsy on a corpse."

"Why?" Marshal McShane blurted out

despite himself. "Why would he do that?"

"How the hell should I know?" Colonel Hendricks grunted. "Figuring out that kind of crap is your job, not mine, Marshal."

"I assure you, I'll be getting right on that," Marshal McShane promised.

"Right," Colonel Hendricks didn't sound as if she really gave a crap. "Regardless, I believe I have indulged you enough about the past. We need to be focused on the present. I have things that need attending to but the chief here will brief you on the current state of this station."

With that, Colonel Hendricks left his office without another word.

"She always that intense?" McShane asked Chief Beckett.

The chief laughed. "I think the colonel likes you, Marshal. She went pretty easy on you just now."

McShane sighed, leaning back in his chair, as he waited for the chief to bring him up to speed on the current state of Pioneer 4.

****

"Here you are, ma'am," the big soldier, Gunther, told Dr. Angela Lowery. "Dr. Jeffery will be in there."

Their walk through the twisting corridors of the Pioneer 4 station had come to an end outside the doors of its main lab. Dr. Lowery could sense that Gunther had no intention of going inside with her and likely wouldn't even if she asked him to.

"Thanks," Dr. Lowery told the giant but he was already walking away and didn't seem to hear her.

She reached out, pressing a thumb to the scanner next to the doors. They opened before her, sliding apart to reveal a large open lab that contained numerous workstations and several operating tables. Its walls were lined with storage shelves and there were sinks on each side of the room. A rail thin, pale man in dark glasses, wearing a surgical mask, stood over the body of a creature which could only be from the Deep Black, happily cutting happily at it with the blade of his scalpel. The thing was surely dead because it didn't respond to the damage being done to its body and wasn't strapped to the top of the table. One of its long, black scale-covered arms dangled from the side of the table. Dr. Lowery saw the razor-like talons of its fingers. She shuddered at the sight of them knowing just how much damage they could inflict upon the flesh of a human in a single swipe. Then the smell of the lab hit her. Dr. Lowery reeled where she stood just inside the doors that had closed behind her. The stench was like rotting tuna, overpowering and sickening. A pained, nauseous moan escaped her lips as she shot out a hand to brace herself against the wall to avoid collapsing from the intensity of what she had breathed in.

"Ah! Dr. Lowery!" the man shouted, looking up from his work on the creature's corpse at the sound of her near collapse. "Who let you in here without a mask?"

Dr. Lowery couldn't answer him. She was still struggling just to breathe in the overpowering stench that filled the lab. The man set aside his scalpel, tugging off his gloves, and rushed to a storage cabinet near him before coming in her direction, carrying a breather unit. Dr. Lowery didn't resist but rather lowered her head to make it easier for the man to slide it over her head. Then she sucked in a deep, uncontaminated breath.

The man helped to steady her as Dr. Lowery recovered.

"Thank you," she croaked weakly.

"You are Dr. Angela Lowery, are you not?" the man asked with a puzzled expression behind the mask he himself wore.

"I am," she answered.

"Then would you care to explain to me why you'd come in here without taking the proper precautions first?" he challenged her.

Dr. Lowery shook her head, clearing it, and stood fully back upright. "I arrived only minutes ago! bHow was I supposed to know what was in this lab? It's not like the big guy who brought me here told me anything!"

"No one from the science staff met you at

the sub dock?" The man's shoulders slumped. "I was sure I told Wallace to meet you there. Well, there's nothing to be done about that now, is there? I hope you'll forgive me for my anger with you, Dr. Lowery. It appears the fault for everything falls solely upon me. Allow me to introduce myself; I am Dr. Allen Jeffery, head of the civilian staff aboard this station."

Dr. Jeffery extended his hand to her. She accepted it and the two of them shook.

"I do tend to get lost in my work here sometimes," Dr. Jeffery admitted. "Often it comes down to me to make sure that our quotas are met. I am the only fully trained surgeon after all or at least I was until your arrival."

Dr. Lowery looked again at the corpse that he'd been working upon as she entered. "You're harvesting the glands of that creature."

Sounding impressed by her quick understanding of things, Dr. Jeffery nodded. "I was indeed. You see, that is where the base material for the drug known as Everlasting truly comes from."

"But. . .but. . .I thought it was being harvested from somewhere in the Deep Black," Dr. Lowery stammered.

"Oh, in the early days of the Pioneer stations it was," Dr. Jeffery assured her. "And that was a terrible mistake. There was no need to waste resources going into the trench itself when the very creatures we needed were coming to us, or rather at us. You see, they know why we are here, Dr. Lowery, and strive to drive us away nearly every day. Those attacks on this station leave the water around it teeming with their corpses, though not always intact, of course. All that needs to be done is to dispatch some mechs and divers to collect them. Once the corpses are brought inside, they are stored in a holding bay until such time as I, or soon you, are able to process them."

Dr. Lowery didn't know what to say. What he was telling her didn't entirely match up with what she had been told to expect.

"You seem surprised by what I have said," Dr. Jeffery clicked his tongue in an annoyed manner. "I understand that the corporation wants to keep the true source of where the material comes from under wraps but even so, one would think they'd better prepare a doctor being sent to extract it."

"Wait," Dr. Lowery stared at Dr. Jeffery. "Are you telling me that this lab produces every single shipment that is sent to the surface?"

"Indeed," Dr. Jeffery chuckled. "The amount which can be extracted from the glands of a single creature is enough to produce hundreds of doses of Everlasting."

Stunned to silence, Dr. Lowery continued to stare at the pale, thin man in front of her.

"I can see that you were expecting much more in terms of a processing plant," Dr.

Jeffery grinned, "But no, it has been just me and will continue to be until I can show you the proper method of gland extraction. Believe you me, Dr. Lowery, one doesn't want one of their glands exploding while you are working on it."

****

The front of Riggs' Silt Stomper hissed open now that the mech was locked in place within its charging dock. The sergeant climbed out of the suit's pilot compartment, leaping to land on the bay floor. Noah, despite being younger, was actually using the docking ladder to climb down from his Silt Stomper.

A young man with thick glasses came walking up to them. Riggs didn't recognize him.

"Sergeant," the kid said to him, "I was told to report to you, sir, once you had returned from your patrol."

"You're the new tech?" Sergeant Riggs didn't quite know what to make of the kid. He sure as hell didn't look like he could have survived Basic much less landed an assignment down here in Pioneer 4.

"Yes sir, specialist Daniel Wrinkler, reporting for duty," the kid stood at attention.

Riggs grunted. "Well don't just stand there then. Get these Stompers serviced and ready for the next patrol."

"Right away, sir," Wrinkler assured him.

Stomach grumbling, Riggs left the new kid to the work he'd assigned him, and kept walking for the doorway that led out of the Silt Stomper hangar bay.

Hurrying to catch up to him, Noah reached his side, keeping pace with Riggs' hurried stride.

"Can you believe that nerd, Sarge?" Noah asked, shaking his head.

"Not every soldier can be a killer, kid," Riggs said. "Without troopers like him, our gear would be falling apart so give the nerd a shot before you go tearing into him. Do I make myself clear?"

"Crystal, sir," Noah answered.

"Now, I don't know about you but I am fragging starving," Riggs snarled. "I'm going to grab some grub. You're welcome to tag along if you want but I don't want to hear any more crap about the new tech or anything else work related."

"Copy that," Noah smirked.

It was more than Riggs' mood that caused him to order Noah to shut up. The military and civilian contingents of the station's crew tended to keep out of each others' way these days but the one place on the station where you could count on finding both was the mess. Everyone who wanted to eat ended up there eventually. Tensions were high enough without Noah mouthing off and maybe making things worse than they already were.

As the two of them entered the mess, Riggs took a look around and saw they had been lucky enough to miss the bulk of the supper crowd. Eph, the civilian cook, was refilling the potato salad on the mess's buffet-like, serve yourself bar. Their fellow Stomper pilots, Becca and Cain, were chowing down at a table in the back of the large room and the giant Gunther sat at a table alone near them while a group of civilians ate at its other side. Riggs knew them all. The group consisted of Mike, Black, and Hammond. Mike and Hammond were little more than grunt labor, well muscled, hardworking, blue collar guys without much of an education to speak of. He'd gotten along with them well until things had gone south on the station. Grunts of all kinds tended to stick together. Even now, Riggs still respected the two men. Black, though, she was anything but simple and served as Pioneer 4's communications officer, something that pained Colonel Hendricks to no end. The colonel believed that job should have been filled by an officer, not some civilian, no matter how qualified or skilled they were.

Picking up a tray, Riggs started down the food line with Noah following after him. Riggs loaded up with a massive burger and a side of fries while Noah snagged pizza and a heaping portion of mac and cheese. Both of them gave a respectful nod to Eph as he passed them on his way back into the kitchen. Civilian or not, Eph was a good guy and it was best not to anger a man who could poison you if he wanted to.

As they finished getting their food, Dr. Jeffery entered the mess. There was a new lady with him that Riggs didn't know. She wore a lab coat though so that said everything that was needed about her. The lady was hot as hell with the right curves in all the places Riggs liked. The nerdiness of how her hair was pulled back and the glasses she wore only added to her appeal. Noah must have shared his opinion of the new lady because the young soldier whistled at her.

"Now see here!" Dr. Jeffery raged, his cheeks flushed red with sudden anger, coming towards them, a finger held out as if he were scolding a pair of misbehaving children. "I will not have my people treated in such a manner, Sergeant!"

The lady held back, uncomfortable, clearly embarrassed by the action on both sides of what was happening in front of her.

"Doc," Riggs warned. "Leave it be. The kid was just blowing off some steam. We just got back from fending off another attack from the Deep Black."

"That's no excuse, Sergeant!" Dr. Jeffery spat. "I will not allow Dr. Lowery to be objectified by that young man or anyone else."

Dr. Jeffery had closed on him and was right

up in Riggs' face.

"Back off, Doc," Riggs retreated a step himself, not wanting the trouble that he could feel in his bones was coming. Mike, Black, and Hammond had gotten to their feet, watching things closely. Becca was just smirking. She and Cain were just trying not to laugh at what was going on.

"I will not back off, Sergeant! Someone needs to put you and your men into their place!" Dr. Jeffery tried to shove Riggs but achieved nothing more than to knock his tray of food from his hands. He stood there looking up into Riggs' eyes, going pale.

"Have it your way then, Doc." Riggs grabbed Dr. Jeffery by the front of his shirt, holding it tight, as his other hand came up, clenched into a fist.

But before Riggs could throw his punch, a man with short cropped, midnight black hair, came sprinting into the mess towards him. He leaped between them, shoving the doc away, sending him stumbling out of Riggs' reach while his other hand slashed through the air. Riggs was barely able to block the man's attack which would have slammed into his throat. He countered with a kick that should have smashed into the new arrival's stomach but the man easily dodged the attack. Frustrated and perplexed, Riggs lashed out again, taking a swing with his right fist. The man turned sideways with impossible speed, Riggs' fist punching through the air where he had been. Riggs cried out in disbelief and pain as the man caught his extended arm, using his own momentum against him to twist it around behind his back. Holding his arm in place where it could almost effortlessly be snapped, the man finally spoke, "That will be quite enough, Sergeant."

"Who the hell are you?" Riggs bellowed.

"I don't care who you are," Riggs heard Gunther growl as the big man rose from his seat and came marching towards them. "Let the Sarge go or I'll break you in half."

"Gunther," Riggs said through teeth clenched against the pain he was in.

The big man paid him no heed, continuing to advance on the stranger.

Riggs felt the man holding his arm shift his stance behind him as he said to Gunther, "I'm not arresting this man but I will throw your arse in the brig if you make me."

"You're McShane," Riggs realized. "The new marshal."

"Guilty as charged," McShane quipped. "Now tell your man there to stand the hell down and I'll let you go."

"I ain't standing down," Gunther raged. "No one hurts the Sarge."

"Listen to him, Gunther," Riggs ordered but the big man, blinded by anger, still wasn't hearing anything he said.

"Fine," McShane sighed, releasing his hold on Riggs. "We'll do this your way, big guy."

Gunther roared and charged the new marshal. McShane was ready for Gunther though, standing his ground and allowing the big man to come to him. The giant swung at McShane, lashing out in a flurry of blows. McShane retreated, ducking, sidestepping, and twisting about to avoid each and every one of them until the giant had over extended himself. Gunther grunted in pain, doubling over, as McShane planted a booted foot in his midsection then smashed an elbow downward into the big man's back. With a heavy thud, Gunther toppled onto the floor.

"Stay the hell down," McShane barked.

The big man still wasn't listening though. Gunther was halfway up from the floor, trying to lunge at the marshal again as McShane's knuckles crashed into his face. The sharp crack of breaking bone seemed to echo in the mess as Gunther's nose broke, his head jerking to the left from the force of McShane's punch. The big man's eyes rolled up to show only white and he fell back onto the floor, unconscious.

"Frag me," Riggs heard Noah mutter. The younger pilot had rushed over to his side as the two of them had watched the new marshal and Gunther go at it. Riggs was impressed, doubting if he could have taken Gunther one on one, much less as easily as Marshal McShane had.

"Anybody else?" McShane asked, looking around the mess.

Not a single soul in the large room spoke up.

"Good," the new marshal said. "Sergeant Riggs, I am going to need you and your man there to carry this big guy to the brig for me."

"Yes sir," Riggs nodded, snapping to attention like the professional he was. While the marshal wasn't his direct commanding officer, he sure as hell outranked a mere mech pilot sergeant.

****

No sooner than Riggs and Noah finished depositing Gunther in the brig and closing the door to his cell behind them as Marshal McShane watched, Colonel Hendricks arrived, storming into the room with them.

"What the hell is the meaning of this, McShane?" Colonel Hendricks challenged him as McShane stood his ground.

"I don't understand what you mean, Colonel," McShane said calmly. "Your man over there in the cell attacked me. I can't overlook that."

"Oh hell yes you could," she protested. "You're letting the sergeant walk, aren't you?"

"I am," McShane nodded, "But I believe I can trust Sergeant Riggs to have learned his lesson. I can't say the same about the big guy."

"Ma'am," Sergeant Riggs tried to cut in but Colonel Hendricks wasn't having it.

"Stow it, Riggs," she silenced him. "We'll talk later."

Whirling back around at Marshal McShane, fuming, Colonel Hendricks snarled, "I want Gunther released right now."

"I am sorry, Colonel, but that's not going to happen," McShane assured her. "You weren't there but the big guy not only attacked me but also disobeyed a direct order from Sergeant Riggs, too."

"That's true, ma'am," Riggs chimed in, despite her warning for him not to. "I did order Gunther to stop."

"Let me ask you something," McShane popped off before she raged at Sergeant Riggs again. "Is this sort of behavior normal for Gunther?"

"What?" Colonel Hendrick sounded as if he had grossly insulted her. "Of course it's not! Gunther is a stand up trooper. I've never had any issue with his performance on this station before."

"Then I'd say something has changed with him," McShane told her. "You weren't there to see the look in his eyes as he came at me or you'd understand exactly why he's in the brig now and not coming out until I say otherwise."

"What are you suggesting, Marshal? That

Gunther has lost it, gone crazy somehow? How the hell would you know that?" Colonel Hendricks demanded. "You haven't even been on this station for twenty-four hours yet."

"I've been reading over Marshal Hershey's reports and. . ." McShane started.

"Not that fragging crap again!" Colonel Hendricks spat. "That man was the one who was fragging crazy! There's nothing strange or weird going on here beyond the normal pressures of living in an environment like Pioneer 4."

"Maybe, maybe not," McShane shrugged. "Time will tell one way or the other. For now though, I've got a ton of paperwork to get done thanks to your man over there," he gestured at Gunther who was still unconscious, lying on the bed of his cell. "So I'd best get to it."

"This isn't over," Colonel Hendricks promised. "I'll be lodging an official complaint. You can count on that."

"That is your right," McShane told her. "Feel free to do so if you like."

Colonel Hendricks huffed and left the brig as angrily as she had entered it, leaving Sergeant Riggs and Noah behind. McShane turned to look at the two pilots. The younger one shared Hendrick's anger and stood glaring at him. The sergeant though seemed not to. Riggs was looking at Gunther where the big man lay in his cell.

"Come on, Sarge," Noah urged. "Let's get out of here."

"You go on," Riggs ordered. "I'll catch up."

Noah hesitated, glancing back at Riggs, but then nodded and left the brig.

"Sergeant," McShane said. "Is there something further I can help you with? Like I told the colonel, I won't be releasing your big friend in there."

"You're not wrong," Riggs sighed. "I mean about Gunther. He wasn't himself in the mess. I saw it too. It was like something inside of him had snapped."

McShane smiled. "Thank you, Sergeant. I'm glad someone from the military side of things here is willing to listen to reason."

Riggs didn't really appear to know how to respond to that comment. "Marshal Hershey was a nut job, sir. There's no denying that. Still, after what I saw in Gunther's eyes today, I have to admit the man might have been onto something."

"So you know about Hershey's theory then?" McShane asked.

"I haven't read the reports like you and the colonel because I don't have that level of clearance," Riggs shrugged. " I know what I have seen though and have overheard a bit here and there in the rumor mill."

"I'll say that for someone who thinks Hershey's theory was just the ravings of a madman, your colonel sure as hell knows a lot about it," McShane commented.

"What are you implying, Marshal?" Riggs grew defensive, the tone of his voice laced with violent warning.

"Nothing. . .yet," McShane assured Riggs. "Tell you what. Why don't you come to my office and you can read over Hershey's reports. It would be nice to have another pair of eyes look them over, maybe point out anything I missed or misunderstood."

"Sure," Riggs grunted, "I can do that."

****

The exterior bay doors opened as Warren and Quin marched out of Pioneer 4 inside their Silt Stompers. There were no current signs of more activity from within the Deep Black. Riggs and Noah had put a quick end to the latest attack. The intervals between attacks varied wildly. Sometimes they came mere hours apart and others, weeks could pass by without more of the creatures swarming out of the deep darkness inside the trench. Warren didn't think they would be seeing any more trouble tonight. She laughed at her own thoughts. Day and night were relative at the bottom of the ocean. They were merely what time told you they were. There was no setting sun or rising moon, only darkness 24-7. After a while it could mess with your head if you let it.

"Where we headed, Warren? Quin asked over their shared commlink.

"Nowhere really," Warren responded. "Everything looks to be quiet out here."

"Were you expecting it not to be?" his sharp voice questioned her.

"Not after an engagement led by Riggs," Warren chuckled. "The Sarge really knows how to kill those bastard things."

Quin snorted, reminding Warren who she was talking to. As good as the Sarge was, Quin was the best fragging Stomper pilot who had ever served at Pioneer 4. The guy was just as much of a killing machine as his mech and just as cold as the metal of its armor too. Before all that crap happened with Marshal Hershey, Quin had been her bet as to who would lose it first. He came across as a sociopath a good bit of the time. Quin only ever seemed to be happy when the guns of his Silt Stomper were blazing or its armored hands crushing the skulls of the creatures from the Deep Black.

"I'll ask again," Quin said. "Where are we heading, Corporal Warren?"

Warren sighed. "Since the trench is quiet, I think a walk around the perimeter would be the best idea, Quin. Check things out and just make sure there are no surprises we don't want lurking around out there."

"As you say." Quin turned his Silt Stomper's course away from the trench and headed westward to start the long trek around Pioneer 4's perimeter there. It wasn't the spot she would have picked to start from but it wasn't worth arguing over so Warren followed after him.

Minutes ticked by as their two mechs marched along, scanning for threats beyond the glow of Pioneer 4's lights. They weren't picking up anything out there in the darkness but Warren felt spooked nonetheless. Something was off but she couldn't put her finger on what it was.

"You see anything out there?" she asked Quin, breaking the silence between them.

His reply was gruff and not more than a single word. "Negative."

Try as she might, Warren couldn't shake the feeling that somehow they, or maybe just she, was in danger. Remembering the day that Marshal Hershey went insane, Warren shuddered despite the controlled temp of the Silt Stomper's sealed environment. That day had been hard on everyone in Pioneer 4. She had been sitting behind Downey at the meeting when Marshal Hershey drew his pistol and shot the poor bastard in the face. The bullet Hershey fired exploded out of Downey's head, drenching her with his blood and brain matter. She was a soldier but Warren did her fighting from inside a massive suit of armor. Downey was her friend so the insides of his head splattering over her had almost been more than she could take.

She'd cried a lot after that. The sense of loss was somehow made more profound for her because of how it happened. Warren had scraped her flesh raw that night and the following few days trying to get the feel of Downey's brain matter off of her. Colonel Hendricks had given her lighter duties while she got her head together but it was really Sergeant Riggs that saved her. Riggs had pulled her out of the depths of despair and hopelessness simply by being the rock that he always was. Watching him go on gave Warren the strength to do so herself. She owed Riggs and for more than just that. When she arrived at Pioneer 4, Riggs had taken her under his wing and helped her to become the pilot that she was. Without his guidance, Warren wouldn't be half the pilot that she was now. Training in simulators was one thing, having someone like Riggs stomping along beside you, barking orders at you while watching over you was quite another.

Warren swept the area beyond the perimeter with her Stomper's sensors again. Still the readings came up clear. There really was nothing out there beyond the light. . . at least that they could detect. The feeling of danger only grew inside Warren though. It was becoming overpowering. Tears welled up in her eyes as Warren tried to shove the fear away inside her mind but failed. Warren looked out of her Silt Stomper to get visual confirmation that Quin was still with her.

"Ma'am?" Quin's voice rang out over her comm. "Why are we holding position here?"

"There's something out there, Quin. I know it," she told him.

"No there's not, ma'am," Quin said forcefully. "Recheck your sensors."

"I have," Warren snarled without mentioning that they only confirmed what he was saying. "But they're wrong, just like you are, Quin."

"Pioneer monitoring," Quin said, no longer talking to her. "This is Stomper X4. Corporal Warren appears to be experiencing some sort of psychological trauma. Please advise."

"What the fragging hell?" Warren raged. "Pioneer, Quin is on the verge of disobeying a direct order. Be informed that I will take whatever action is needed to prevent him from endangering the station."

All Warren heard in response was a sharp crackle of static through her comm.

"Quin, remain in position where you are," she snapped as his Stomper began moving, heading on along the perimeter lighting around the station. Then everything went to hell. Alarms started flashing and beeping at Warren from her suit's tactical display. Something was out there just like she'd thought. Her Stomper's sensors were registering movement in the dark waters beyond the reach of the station's lights. . . and whatever was moving out there, it was fragging large as hell. Warren had never seen anything like the readings she was picking up before. She looked to see that Quin wasn't reacting at all to whatever was out there. His Stomper continued to calmly walk on away from her own in the direction they had been headed in.

"Pioneer 4," Warren yelled, "We've got an incoming contact. Be advised, whatever it is, it's massive!"

Quin's Stomper suddenly turned around to face her own. Her comm was crackling like hell at her, the static coming through it growing louder and louder. Warren wondered if whatever was out there in the darkness was somehow jamming the comms. She didn't have the time to worry about that though, whatever was coming had to be stopped. The shoulder mounted needle guns of her Stomper spun up, sending streams of fire slashing into the darkness towards the direction of the contact her sensors had picked up.

Warren couldn't tell if her fire was hitting anything out there or not. Her Stomper's sensors showed the contact still closing fast. Her eyes cut sideways as Warren noticed movement to her right. Quin's Stomper was running towards hers. What the hell was the idiot doing? She cursed inside her head. Why wasn't he trying to stop the approaching contact too? Warren sucked in a deep breath as she realized that Quin's Stomper was about to plow into hers. She didn't dare stop shooting into the darkness, besides, he was too close now to even attempt dodging. Metal clanged against metal in the water as Quin slammed into her. The impact shook Warren about inside her Stomper despite her pilot's harness. The right hand of Quin's Stomper grabbed hold of one of her suit's shoulder guns, crushing it.

"Pioneer 4!" Warren screamed, knowing her transmission likely wouldn't be heard by the station through the raging static of the comms. "Quin has lost it! He's attacking me! I repeat! Quin is attacking me!"

The remaining shoulder gun of her Stomper couldn't angle around enough to fire at Quin. She had no choice but to engage him directly, given how close he was to her. Warren had learned a long time ago that you didn't mess around in a fight. You struck to do maximum damage and put down your enemy or you risked your own life. Popping her Stomper's left arm blade, Warren thrust it at Quin. He was the better pilot and Warren knew she needed to take him out fast or she was dead. Quin's Stomper shifted to avoid the blade as he lashed out with an armored fist. It smashed her remaining shoulder cannon, rendering it useless.

Warren's Stomper staggered backwards in retreat. The only way to combat Quin was to put some space between them and get a chance to recover before he struck again. Quin wasn't going to let her do that, though. His Stomper lunged forward, smashing into hers again. Her comm was still crackling loudly with furious static even over the echoes of clanging metal that were ringing in her ears but she tried it anyway.

"Stand down!" Warren ordered Quin. "That's an order, damn it!"

Quin knew exactly where to hit her Stomper to disable it, popping one of his own arm blades and plunging into the relays above her power cell. The systems of Warren's Stomper went offline, leaving her helpless as the tactical display before her eyes went dark.

****

Warren woke up in Pioneer 4's med bay. Its harsh, bright lights made her blink and squint as she opened her eyes. McShane felt pity for her as Warren became aware that she was strapped to the bed and went wild in a frenzy of grunting and straining, trying to break free.

Dr. Lowery rushed to the side of Warren's bed, attempting to calm the Stomper pilot down.

"Warren!" Dr. Lowery barked. "Snap out of it! You're safe now!"

The Stomper pilot wasn't hearing her though or maybe couldn't. Warren's eyes were wide with terror. She kept screaming.

"No!" Warren bellowed. "Stay back! Get

away from me!"

Having no other choice left to her, Dr. Lowery shot her up with a powerful sedative. It worked almost instantly. Warren's rage bled away as she slipped back into unconsciousness.

McShane wasn't the only one watching Warren. Colonel Hendricks and her fellow pilot Quin, who had returned her to Pioneer 4, were with him.

"What the hell happened to her out there?" Quin asked and then realized that he had spoken out of place, swallowing hard, as the colonel glared at him.

"I don't know. Whatever is wrong, it isn't physical," Dr. Lowery said.

Colonel Hendricks sighed heavily. "Doctor. . ."

"Colonel, at this point, there's nothing I can do for her beyond keep her from hurting herself or anyone else," Dr. Lowery said.

"Understood," Colonel Hendricks nodded.

McShane saw that Hendricks wasn't any happier with the doctor's answer than he was.

"Is there anything else you can tell us, Mr. Quinn?" he asked, frowning at the Stomper pilot.

Quinn shook his head. "I've already given a full report to Colonel Hendricks."

"That's not what I asked," McShane pressed.

"What is it you're hoping he'll say, Marshall?" Colonel Hendricks took a step towards him.

"Something. . . anything useful that might help us prevent this from happening again," McShane stood his ground.

"Sometimes people just go bonkers down here," Colonel Hendricks shrugged.

"Yes, they do. This is a harsh environment for anyone, I'll concede that. Colonel, but even so, things don't add up," McShane told her.

"Is that so?" Colonel Hendricks locked her eyes with his, scowling.

"You know it is," McShane nodded. "There have been not only more but more violent incidents aboard this station than the numbers predict there should be."

"Marshal," Colonel Hendricks said firmly, "My people have work to do. I won't stand for you stopping them from it to chase crazy theories like your predecessor did. Do I make myself clear?"

"You can't order me around, Colonel," McShane kept his expression and tone calm. "In fact, in matters like this, you're technically under my command."

"Don't you throw the regulations at me, Marshal," Colonel Hendricks warned. "You've pushed me far enough already. Come along, Quinn. We're finished here."

Marshal McShane and Dr. Lowery were left alone in the med bay with Warren. The sedatives had done their job well on the troubled Stomper pilot. She was unconscious and no longer thrashing about. Still, McShane could see Warren's eyes darting about beneath their closed lids.

"I'm beginning to regret taking this job," Dr. Lowery commented.

"You and me both," McShane chuckled.

"I bet so," Dr. Lowery said. "My boss is a touch. . .eccentric to say the least."

"I am beginning to think everyone here is," McShane agreed.

"I don't envy you," Dr. Lowery shook her head. "That Colonel isn't someone I'd want to lock horns with."

McShane shrugged. "I've dealt with worse."

"Really?" Dr. Lowery shot him a disbelieving look before walking over to the workstation her laptop was sitting on.

Changing the subject, McShane asked, nodding his head in the direction of Warren, "There's really nothing physically wrong with her?"

"Not that I can find," Dr. Lowery answered.

McShane sighed. "Then it has to be psychological, right?"

"That would be my thought too," Dr. Lowery said.

"I'd ask if you had seen any signs leading to this apparently sudden break but. . ." McShane started.

"But I just got here too," Dr. Lowery

managed a grin.

"Well, I suppose, let me know if you find out anything more," McShane ordered and headed for the door.

"Will do," he heard Dr. Lowery say before the door to the med bay hissed shut behind him.

****

"Watch it," Becca warned Cain. His Stomper was dangerously close to the mouth of the Deep Black. He'd marched right up to it without fear. Becca wasn't worried about the creatures coming up to attack them. She had done a full sensor sweep of the Deep Black as they approached it which came up clear and then scanned the surrounding area too. There wasn't a sign of the creatures anywhere within the range of her Stomper's sensors. What worried her was that the ground would give way and Cain's Stomper would vanish, tumbling downwards into the darkness of the Deep Black.

"Ha," Cain snorted over the commlink they shared. "Take it easy, boss lady. I'm not as stupid as I look. . . not that you can see me inside of this thing."

"Just come away from the edge, Cain," Becca urged. "Careful or not, you're making me nervous."

Cain's Silt Stomper backpedaled away from the edge of the Deep Black. "Fine."

"What the heck were you doing, anyway?" Becca asked.

"Taking a peek into the dark, I guess," Cain answered. "Don't you ever wonder what's down there?"

"We know what's down there," Becca said. "Those fragging creatures, some freaky fish, and salt water."

Cain laughed. "You sure about that, boss?"

"Where the frag is this coming from, Cain?" Becca shook her head inside her mech.

"In case you haven't taken a look around lately, Becca, things have kind of gone to hell in a handbasket down here," Cain told her. "What happened with Warren. . . that crap wasn't right. You can't tell me Warren wasn't okay before she stepped into her mech that last time."

"We've all been a bit fragged up since. . ." Becca realized she couldn't say the rest out loud.

"Yeah, that's sure as frag the truth," Cain grunted over the comm.

"Looks like we're gonna have to drop this crap for now," Becca told Cain as her suit's tactical display lit up.

"What the frag?" Cain stammered, "Where the hell did they come from?"

Dozens of creatures were closing in on them fast and not a single one had emerged from the depths of the Deep Black.

"It's an ambush!" Becca shouted, knowing

she shouldn't panic. Their two Silt Stompers should be able to handle the number of creatures they were up against with ease. What scared her was the fact that her suit's sensors hadn't picked the things up until they were nearly on top of them and that the creatures weren't coming from out of the trench. That's where they had always shown up from before.

The shoulder guns of Cain's mech opened fire on the monsters. High powered rounds ripped into them, black blood erupting into the water as their exploding bodies blew apart.

Becca saw it was too late to engage the things with her own shoulder guns. They were too close. She popped the arm blades of her Stomper and shifted the mech into a defensive stance. Lashing out with her right arm blade, Becca sliced one of the monsters in half, diagonally along its upper body. The two halves flew away from each other even as she struck again, this time with her left arm blade. The blade cut through the neck of another monster, severing its head from its shoulders. Then the others behind those two plowed into her. They slammed into her Silt Stomper like a rain of human-sized bullets.

The heavy mecha stumbled backwards, barely maintaining its footing as one creature after another thudded into its armor. Each of them held on once they struck, scaled hands grasping, razor-like talons clawing. Becca wasn't having it though. Any panic she had felt was gone now replaced by a growing anger and determination to do her job. Her Stomper shook, like a dog trying to dry itself, flinging most of the creatures from it. A metal hand grabbed the neck of one of the three remaining creatures, yanking it from where it clutched her Stomper's shoulders, breaking its teeth on steel. That hand held it while Becca put her mech's other hand through its head. The creature's head burst like a rotten melon from the force of the blow she dealt it. The rest of the creatures she was engaged with had recovered from being flung from her Stomper and swarmed around it, striking vainly at the mech with their taloned hands. Kicking her Stomper's systems up to full power and redlining it, Becca charged forward away from the creatures. There was no running from the things. They were born to these depths, darting about with ease whereas her Stomper was more akin to a tank, built for endurance and power, not speed. A creature came streaking up on her left flank. Becca planted an elbow in its chest, shattering the bones of the creature's ribs. Its body went limp, floating upwards as the legs of her Stomper kept pumping, charging onward. Huge amounts of silt were thrown into the water from each step her mech took. Not that it mattered. The creatures could somehow see through it just as easily as her Stomper's sensors could.

The shoulder guns of Cain's Stomper had fallen silent. The things had closed on him like they had her earlier. He was engaging them hand to claws. The arm blades of his Stomper were extended and already smeared with the sticky, foul black blood of the monsters. Pieces of slashed up creatures floated around the battle that was ensuing. Cain heard the screeching noise of a particularly strong set of claws being dragged against the side of his Stomper's head. Fresh adrenaline surged through his body. A creature thudded into the back of his mech. Cain realized instantly that the thing wasn't trying to just knock him off balance. No. It was trying to pry off the armor plating that covered his Stomper's power cell. What the hell? he wondered. It was like the thing had suddenly grown a brain.

"Becca!" Cain shouted, calling out for help over the comm. A quick glance at his tactical display told him that there would be no help coming from her though. She was in the thick of it too, engaged with her own group of creatures. Cain heard the hash groan of metal bending as two more creatures joined the first, sinking their clawed fingers into the small breach it had created, adding their strength to tearing the plating loose. Spinning his Stomper around, Cain tried desperately to get his hands on the creatures or at least get them away from what they were doing. He managed to close the armored fingers of his right hand around the leg of one of the creatures. With maximum strength his Stomper could generate, Cain whipped the monster through the water, slamming it into the ocean floor. There was a sharp crack of bone that accompanied the muted thud of the impact as the creature's neck bent at an unnatural angle. Cain let go of the dead creature, making a grab at another. It streaked easily out of his reach. A flash of light filled his eyes so bright he had to clench them shut against it. The shriek of a whine that died down in volume almost as fast as it arose stung his ears. Then there was only darkness and silence.

Severing the arm from a creature with her left arm blade, the right arm blade of Becca's Stomper thrust outward, impaling another. Wrenching the right blade free, Becca allowed herself a smile. There were only a few of the creatures she was engaged with remaining. The now one armed creature was screeching, or as close to that as one did underwater. Becca retracted her arm blades, grabbing the thing, sinking the armored fingers of her Stomper into the center of its chest. Without effort, she ripped open its ribcage, loosing an explosion of black blood.

Becca had heard Cain cry out over the commlink. There had been fear, real fear, in his voice. Becca wondered what in the hell could scare an experienced pilot like him until she turned and saw that his Stomper was down. Her heart skipped a beat at the sight of it. Then things got worse. The armor plating covering the Stomper's power cell was torn away. Exposed, nearly shredded wiring, spilled out.

"Cain!" Becca yelled, already knowing on some level that even if he was still alive, there would be no answer. From the amount of damage done to his Stomper, she could clearly see it was offline. Becca's Stomper launched forward, charging across the ocean floor towards where Cain's Stomper lay face down in the silt. As she closed the distance, her Stomper's targeting system locked onto the creatures in the water around the collapsed mech. She opened fire, shoulder guns blazing. Half of the creatures that remained from the ones who had engaged Cain died instantly, ripped to shreds by the high velocity needles tearing through them. The rest of the creatures scattered, darting away in different directions trying to avoid the death that had claimed their brethren. It did them no good. Her shoulder guns tracked and obliterated them anyway.

Becca's Stomper slowed as it approached Cain's. She couldn't come to a sudden stop in the water without risking sending herself flying. Physics didn't work the same way at the bottom of the ocean as they did on land. As her Stomper came to a halt, Becca increased power to its sensors, scanning Cain's downed mech.

They were picking up life-signs inside the powerless armor and it appeared to be intact other than the power core systems. Becca let out a sigh of relief. Cain was still alive. Becca knew her Stomper could drag his home as long as she was careful not to overheat her own systems doing it. It would take some time but Cain should have plenty of air as she could tell the emergency life support had kicked in after his Stomper's main power had been knocked out.

"Stomper patrol to Pioneer 4," Becca said over her comm. "We've got a downed mech out here."

"What the . . ?" she heard Chief Beckett's stunned voice respond. "What the devil happened out there, Becca? We're not getting anything but calm readings from the Deep Black."

"We were attacked. . . ambushed," Becca answered.

"But. . .that doesn't make any sense," Chief Beckett said.

"The creatures that hit us didn't come of the trench, Beckett," she told him. "They came at us from beyond the perimeter lighting of the station."

The commlink was silent. Becca could picture the disbelieving look on the chief's face.

"You sound calm," Chief Beckett commented at last. "I assume the battle is over and Cain is still alive."

"It is. The bastards have been properly fragged." Becca heard the chief chuckle at her choice of words. "As to Cain, I think he's okay. His suit is offline but intact. Just going to be hell getting him home."

"Roger that," Chief Beckett chuckled. "Do you require assistance?"

"Nah," Becca replied. "I can get it done. I'll let you know if I run into any trouble."

"Copy that, but I am dispatching another patrol anyway," Chief Beckett informed her. "We need to have eyes out there if those things really came at you from somewhere other than the Deep Black."

"They did," Becca assured the chief.

"Get back to the station as fast as you can, Becca," Chief Beckett told her. "And be careful while you're doing it. God only knows how many more of those things could be lurking out there in the dark."

****

"No," Specialist Wrinkler croaked, standing his ground, as Sergeant Riggs towered over him. Quin was there too. The lethal little man's beady eyes were locked onto the kid and the low rumble of a growl rose up his throat.

"Kid," Sergeant Riggs warned, "I ain't got time for this crap. We've got a downed Stomper out there."

"Sir," Wrinkler said, "the Stompers you two are taking out haven't finished charging up yet. If you take them out and. . ."

"Don't make us move you, Wrinkler," Quin snarled. "It won't be gentle if you force us to."

"Quin!" Riggs snapped. "Watch it. He's on our side."

"Yes sir," Quin frowned.

"Look, Wrinkler, I know those Stompers aren't up to full power but this isn't a normal situation. We need to be out there right now so you're going to step aside and help us get those mechs into the water," Riggs told the young trooper. "There are pilots out there that need us."

Wrinkler swallowed hard as it appeared as if Riggs' words had sunk in. The nerdy Stomper tech sprang into action. "Go get into your Stompers," he told them. "I'll get you out there A.S.A.P."

Riggs gave the young tech a nod of approval as they parted, heading in different directions. He and Quin climbed the separate ladders to get suited up. Riggs slid into the pilot compartment of his Stomper and felt its safety harness come to life, hugging tightly against his chest and legs. His fingers flipped a series of switches bringing the Stomper completely online as its metal armor closed up around him, sealing him within it.

Word was that Becca and Cain were okay.

Riggs wasn't really worried about them but he was concerned. It was rare that a Stomper took enough damage to knock it offline and clearly whatever battle had taken place out there, it hadn't been on that kind of scale. The chief had used the word ambush and that stuck with Riggs. He had never known the creatures from the Deep Black to show the kind of intelligence it took to plan something like that against two Silt Stompers. Supposedly, the area around Pioneer 4 was clear of the creatures now but Riggs had his doubts. God only knew what he and Quin were headed into.

He and Quin had worked together before. It wasn't that large of a station and there were only six Stomper pilots in total, to keep it safe. They got on well enough on a professional level. Riggs didn't really care for Quin though. He was a born killer. Riggs had known plenty like him before, people who signed up to fight just so they could kill. Quin loved his gig here at Pioneer 4. The constant battles with the creatures from the Deep Black really seemed to make him come alive. Sometimes it almost made Quin smile, no small feat considering how cold the bastard was.

"All systems green and ready for exit," Riggs heard Quin report over the comm. as the killer's Stomper stepped out of its charging station.

"Sergeant?" Wrinkler's voice asked.

"All systems green here too," Riggs confirmed. "Ready to get moving."

"Roger that," Wrinkler responded.

The two Silt Stompers marched across the bay towards the airlock that would release them in the ocean beyond Pioneer 4's thickly armored walls. The massive doors parted to allow them to enter and then closed behind them. Water poured into the airlock as the pressure adjusted and stabilized.

"Clear for exit," Wrinkler called out as the doors the two Stompers now faced inside the lock opened and then they were moving again, stepping out onto the ocean floor.

"Bringing sensors online to full operational power," Quin said over the comm.

Riggs already had his suit's up and running. He swept the darkness beyond the reach of the lights around Pioneer 4's perimeter. Nothing. As far as the sensors were concerned, there wasn't anything lurking around to be a threat to them.

"Got eyes on Becca," Quin called out.

Looking past his tactical display, Riggs saw her Stomper too. It was moving slowly towards the station, lurching along, dragging Cain's damaged Stomper behind her. Huge waves of stirred up silt obscured everything beyond her position.

"Becca, Sergeant Riggs and Quin here. We've come to relieve you," Riggs said.

"Do you require assistance?" Quin asked.

"Negative on that," Becca responded as a crackle of static ran through all their comms. There was an edge of amusement in her voice.

"Something funny?" Riggs frowned, wondering what she was on about.

"Just surprised it's the two of you. You know the crap has really hit the fan when they send both of you out together," Becca smirked inside her Stomper.

"They didn't send us. We volunteered," Sergeant Riggs told her. "I needed to make sure you and Cain were safe. As for Quin there, you know he'll take any chance to frag up some of those creatures that he can get."

"Movement!" Quin suddenly barked, the shoulder guns of his Stomper craning upwards as the heavy mech whirled about.

"Stand down," Sergeant Riggs ordered. "That's just today's launch."

And it was. The upper bay of the Pioneer 4 station had opened, dispatching the automated transport shuttle that would carry the latest shipment of harvested genetic material to the surface.

They all stood watching as the transport slowly rose up and away from Pioneer 4. Due to the delicate nature of its contents, the transport *had to* ascend slowly.

Then without warning, things went utterly to hell around them. Layers of silt erupted into the water as previously motionless creatures leaped up from the ocean floor already within melee range of the Stompers. They weren't the only creatures. More of the things came swimming towards the station from the dark waters beyond the station's perimeter and even more were streaming out of the mouth of the Deep Black.

Claws raked over the reinforced glass of the eye slits of Riggs' Stomper. He flinched but managed not to make the heavy mech stumble backwards. There wasn't a chance in hell of anyone being able to use their shoulder guns until they cleared out the creatures that were already on them. Riggs' armored hands grabbed a creature and bent its top half backwards until its spine snapped.

"Yeah! That's right!" Quin was shouting. "Bring it, you mothers!"

Riggs didn't have a visual on Quin or Becca. There were too many creatures swarming in the water between them. Riggs could see them both on his tactical display however and Cain's damaged Stomper too. He thanked God that at least the monsters were leaving Cain alone for now. A loud thud rattled his Stomper as a pair of creatures struck at its faceplate in front of his eyes. A tiny crack appeared in the reinforced glass and Riggs knew he needed to act fast. If he didn't, he was as good as dead. The pressure at this depth alone would kill him before he could even drown if his Stomper was breached.

Pumping all the power his suit could muster into the servos of its legs, Riggs hurled his Stomper forward. It plowed through the swarming creatures, charging clear of them.

Quin was having a blast. He crushed the skull of one creature, ripped the arm off another, and then used that arm to smash in still another's face, bludgeoning it again and again with the severed limb. Creatures slashed vainly at his Stomper with their claws, failing to do any greater damage than scratching its paint. Quin fought like a madman high on the blood that he was spilling.

Becca had been knocked off balance when the things first shot up from beneath the silt. Her Stomper had toppled over, crashing onto its back. She looked up through its eye slits into the mass of creatures above her as they fought desperately to tear and pry their way to her inside the heavy mech. Getting her Stomper back up wouldn't have been an easy task even if she weren't under attack. With so many of the creatures clinging to it and trying to keep the mech pinned down, it was impossible. All she could do was try to fight back from where she was. Her Stomper's arm blades were already extended and Becca slashed wildly at the creatures with them. Black blood spilled into the water as creatures died shrieking. For each one of the creatures that Becca killed or injured enough to take out of the fight, another took its place.

Riggs had managed to get out of the mass of swarming creatures. Looking back, he still couldn't see any of the others. Just opening up with his shoulder guns on the swarm of creatures was far too risky. Firing blind, he was likely to hit Becca or Quin. The needles they fired traveled with such velocity and power, if they hit a Stomper just right, they could do some serious damage. Part of him wanted to charge back into the chaotic melee but Riggs knew that wouldn't help anyone. He needed a plan, something that would clear the creatures out and off the others. There weren't exactly a lot of options. Hell, in truth, Riggs couldn't think of a single one.

Cain continued his battle with the creatures around him, drinking in every glorious moment of the violence and gore. His right arm blade thunked into the skull of a creature. Cain watched the thing twitching from the damage to its brain for a fraction of a second before yanking the weapon free. He didn't feel threatened at all by the monsters around him. The stabilizing drills of his Stomper were extended, bracing his mech where it was, with no chance of it being knocked over no matter how many of the creatures slammed into him or from what angle. He knew, too, that the claws and teeth of the creatures weren't really capable of piercing his Stomper's armor either. Cain had it made. The way Cain saw things was that his Stomper stood in the center of a killing field and all the creatures were his to dispose of as he liked. Cain stabbed a creature through its chest. The thrust alone killed the thing but Cain angled his blade as it was yanked free so that the weapon cut its body apart. The entire area around him was black, almost as much the blood of the creatures as it was water now, but he could still see effectively thanks to the vision enhancements his Stomper gave him. Cain lashed out again, his left arm blade relieving a creature of its leg at the hip. The monster shrieked in pain before he finished it by bringing his right arm blade around to take its head. Cain was grinning like a blood drunk vampire inside his Stomper as he suddenly retracted its arm blades. There were still creatures all about him but Cain was having so much fun that he wanted to kick it up a notch. *You only live once,* Cain thought, switching the means of how he was fighting to a much more hands on approach. His Stomper shifted into a pose similar to that of a boxer's stance. Cain threw one punch after another, each shattering bones and adding more black blood to the cloud around him.

Having just ended the life of a creature by opening up its ribs with a slash of an arm blade, Becca sucked in a breath as a chill ran through her body. She had no idea where it had come from. Sweat was glistening on her flesh from the exertion of the battle and the toll it was taking on her. Her Stomper's systems remained fully functional and as thus its interior environment uncompromised. The internal temperature was just as stable as it had been when the battle began. No, there was no explanation she could come up with for what she was feeling as a chill shot through her again. She kept fighting, keeping the creatures from maintaining enough of a hold on her Stomper to do it any real damage. For the briefest of seconds, her vision blurred. It snapped back to normal even as she loosed a scream that echoed inside the pilot compartment around her. Something terrible and primal forced its way into her mind. Not physically but on a mental level unlike anything Becca had ever experienced before. There were no words to describe it. It was the ultimate feeling of violation. The arms of her Stomper stopped their frantic slashing as Becca squealed in fear. She thrashed about in the safety harness that was supposed to protect her from impacts, battling the unseen force that had ripped its way into her head. Her fear was a crazed, all consuming panic. The creatures above her Stomper seized the moment, several of them slamming onto it. Their fingers searched and probed for places to get a firm get on the crevices of the armor, trying to rend them open.

"No!" Becca yelled at the top of her lungs, activating her Stomper's shoulder guns. They opened fire, upwards, into and through the creatures. The ones right on top of her in the guns' line of fire splattered apart in bursts of black blood, fragments of bone, and gore.

"What the hell?" Riggs shouted as he saw streams of needle fire erupt out of the swarm of creatures. His breath caught in his throat as Riggs realized where the needles were headed. . . and there wasn't a fragging thing he could do to stop them.

The raising, automated transport was struck by the continuing streams of high velocity needle fire. They cut a swath of destruction across its hull. The transport rolled leftward though Riggs couldn't tell if its automated systems were attempting evasive maneuvers or if they had been knocked offline entirely and it was merely drifting in that direction. That question never got answered because. . . the transport blew before Riggs' eyes. It went up in a bright flash of flames and heat. Jagged pieces of debris spun away from the explosion, rolling through the water.

"Frag," Riggs cursed, bracing for the shockwave he knew was coming. A couple of pieces of debris clanged off his Stomper's arms as Riggs raised them to block any that came his way. Then the shockwave hit in their wake. It rocked his Stomper, jarring him inside of the mech. Riggs rode it out and then ran a quick diagnostic check on his suit's systems. Everything checked out green.

One good thing, the shockwave had scattered the creatures that had been swarming around the others. Those that weren't too greatly injured or outright killed by it were on the run, darting away back towards the darkness they had come from. Riggs powered up his Stomper's shoulder guns, using his suit's targeting system, shredding as many of the creatures as he could with bursts of high velocity needles as they fled. Quin was whooping and hollering like a kid who had just won the biggest game of war in his life. His Stomper was coated in the foul, black sticky blood of God only knew how many creatures.

Becca felt the presence of whatever had grasped her mind leave her. Her fear subsided but didn't go away. She was shaken to her core. It took a moment for her to fully realize that she was alone inside of her head again and even then, it was hard to focus. Looking out of her Stomper, there was no sign of the monsters above her, trying to tear their way in, anymore. A feeling of dread loomed over her as fresh, new chills of a different origin coursed through her bones. Becca shook her head as best she could in her safety harness, trying to clear it and get her focus back. She could hear Riggs shouting over the comm. Something was up and it wasn't anything good.

"Holy. . ." Chief Beckett's voice rang out through the commlink. "What the hell? Did someone really just shoot up the transport?"

"Roger that," Riggs confirmed gruffly. "The transport is gone."

"Gone?" Chief Beckett asked as if he was still trying to believe it.

"Blown to hell," Riggs snapped. "Needle fire must have punched its power cells. They went up like fireworks under a match out here."

"Oh my . . ." Chief Beckett started but Riggs interrupted him.

"We've got two Stompers down now," the Sergeant snarled. "Things appear clear for the moment but I don't know how long that's going to last."

Wrinkler's voice cut into the commlink. "I've been monitoring things from here in the bay. I've got the other Stompers priming for launch."

"Belay that," Sergeant Riggs ordered. "The last thing we need is more people out here right now."

"Sergeant, I'm not sure that's your call to make," Chief Beckett protested.

"I'm the ranking officer in the field so it sure as hell is, Chief," Riggs roared. "You send out more Stompers and I'll tear you a new one when I get in there."

"Understood," Chief Beckett answered with

both anger and defeat in his voice. "But be advised that Colonel Hendricks is on her way to the CIC."

"Copy that," Riggs grunted. "Wrinkler, get ready. We're coming in with damaged mechs in tow."

Riggs turned his attention to Quin. "Hey man, get your head out of your arse and give me a hand here. The battle's over."

"Yes sir," Quin responded.

Becca felt tears welling up in her eyes as her Stomper slowly, awkwardly, rose up from the ocean floor. The sight of Cain's Stomper was almost too much for her. The creatures had torn into it, cracking the heavy suit open through the strength of their sheer numbers.

"You okay?" Sergeant Riggs asked over the comm. as his Stomper came marching up to her own.

"Cain is dead," Becca said simply.

"I can see that," Riggs sighed. "I asked about you."

Becca didn't answer him but Riggs gathered that her Stomper was functional enough to return to Pioneer 4 without needing assistance from him.

"I hate to say it, Becca, but you're going to have a lot to answer for," Riggs warned. "What. . . What do you mean?" Becca stammered, barely hearing what he was saying. She was still shaking despite the act of being okay she was trying to put on.

"You shot the hell out of the transport, Becca," Riggs said.

She spun her Stomper around to fully face his. "I did what?"

"You blew the transport to bits, Becca," Riggs told her again.

"Oh fragging crap," Becca sucked in a startled breath.

"Forget about it for now," Riggs ordered. "We've got to get everyone inside before more creatures show up. None of us are in a state to deal with those things again right now."

"Speak for yourself," Quin chuckled. "I'd love to go another round."

"You're only proving my point for me, man," Riggs huffed. "Calm your ass down and help me with what's left of Cain's suit."

As their two Stompers lifted the battered, ripped open remains of Cain's mech, Becca watched them, wondering how things had all gone so horridly wrong. Everything was so fragged up. . . including her. She didn't remotely understand whatever had happened to her. Nothing made sense about it. Hell, nothing was even rational about it. Wishing she could wipe away the sweat on her brow, Becca had no idea what she was going to say when Colonel Hendricks started hammering her with questions. Becca knew that if she had really shot up the transport like Riggs said, her career was likely over. She might even find herself in the brig before the day was done.

"Come on, Becca, get moving," Sergeant Riggs' gruff voice urged her. "Sticking around out here is a bad idea. Let's get inside while we can."

The mechs entered the exterior airlock together, its huge doors shutting behind them. As the interior lock emptied of water to allow them entrance into the bay proper, Becca gnawed nervously at her lower lip. She felt raw and wound up tight. It was hard to pilot her Stomper into its hold. The armor of her suit clanged against the metal walls more than once. Gasping for air like a drowning woman, Becca leaped out of her Stomper as soon as its chest slid open to allow her out. She saw the new Stomper tech, Wrinkler, running towards her, a deeply concerned expression on his face.

"You okay?" he asked, stopping just short of reaching out to try to steady her. Becca was glad he had or she might have unintentionally grabbed his arm and broken it.

"Except for people asking me that over and over," Becca raged though even Wrinkler, newbie that he was, could tell she was lying.

The door of the corridor leading out of the Stomper bay swished open. Colonel Hendricks entered accompanied by the two new privates, Duffman and Steward. Hendricks looked around the bay carefully assessing the situation.

"Ma'am," Wrinkler snapped to attention as he was the closest to where she'd entered from.

Riggs and Becca stood in front of her damaged Stomper. Quin was just to their left.

"At ease, Wrinkler," Colonel Hendricks said. "I'm not here for you."

Everyone knew exactly who the colonel had come for.

Riggs moved between her and Becca. "Colonel. . .Wait."

"Get out of my way, Sergeant," Colonel Hendricks growled. "I won't ask again."

"It's okay," Becca placed a hand on Riggs' shoulder and gently pushed him aside. "What I did is on me."

"Damn straight it is, girl," Colonel Hendricks spat. "Your screw up has likely just cost us all our arses. What the hell were you thinking blowing up the transport?"

"I . . . I didn't mean to, ma'am," Becca stammered. "I don't know. . .what happened."

"Well you're going to have to do better than that," Colonel Hendricks snarled. "Duffman, Steward, take her to the brig. If she tries to resist, make her pay for it."

"Yes ma'am," Duffman barked, motioning for Becca to put out her hands. As she did so, Steward stepped forward and locked restraints in place over them.

"Colonel!" Riggs challenged her. "Are those really necessary?"

"Last I checked, I was in command aboard this station, Sergeant Riggs," Colonel Hendricks answered him. "And you're out of line. Step out one more time and you'll be joining Becca in the brig."

"I'll be taking this to the Marshal," Riggs told her, standing his ground. "You can't stop me from that."

"Run and tell McShane whatever you want, Sergeant," Colonel Hendricks snorted. "I don't give a fragging crap."

****

McShane sat in his office going through what he'd been able to recover of Dr. Milner's work. . . what there was left of it in the station's computer system anyway. It seemed almost as if someone had accessed the files and tried to censor them. Outright deleting them would have been too obvious and alerted those funding the station that something was up. McShane was on his second read through of the files as the door to his office was slammed inward. He looked up to see Sergeant Riggs, out of breath and sweating, in the doorway.

"Marshal!" Riggs shouted as soon as he'd sucked enough wind back into his lungs to be able to. "I need your help. It's Becca."

He hadn't met Becca yet, not really, and asked, "The pilot who was in the mess during the crap that went down with your man

Gunther?"

Riggs nodded. "Yep. That was her. Colonel Hendricks has taken her into custody and is currently throwing her in the brig."

McShane's eyes went wide. "What the hell? Why didn't anyone call me?"

"Guess the Colonel didn't want you involved, Marshal," Riggs told him. "But I came to get you anyway. The Stompers on patrol were attacked today. We lost a pilot and Becca destroyed the transport that was leaving Pioneer 4 for the surface."

"Frag," McShane muttered, knowing full well just how much the loss of the transport was going to tick off the people funding the station. He had to force himself to remain calm. "Still, I don't see why you're coming to me. It sounds like your Colonel has things in hand."

"Because, Marshal, I don't think she intends to stop at just throwing Becca in the brig." Riggs wiped at the sweat on his brow with the back of his hand. "I think she's going to do a lot worse to Becca before she's done and you're the only one with the power to stop her."

"Becca is under her command and authority," McShane reminded the sergeant.

"I know that, McShane!" Riggs bellowed. "But you're the law on this station, aren't you?"

McShane sighed, seeing that Riggs really believed Colonel Hendricks was going to cross the line with whatever she had planned for

Becca. He got up from behind his desk. "Fine."

"You'll save Becca then?" Riggs asked.

"I can't get her out of the brig," McShane answered honestly. "Colonel Hendricks is well within her power to lock Becca up there. I can however make sure nothing else happens to your friend, Sergeant."

"Thank God," Riggs relaxed, his entire posture shifting. "And thank you, Marshal."

"Sure," McShane shrugged. "Let's go get this over with."

"I can't go with you," Riggs stopped just outside of the door as they left McShane's office. "Me being there will just make things worse."

McShane sighed again. "Kind of figured that. Get back to whatever it is that you're supposed to be doing right now, Sergeant. I got this."

****

Noah returned to his quarters. Like most everyone else in Pioneer 4's military contingent, he'd been sent scrambling into action as the crap with Becca and the others went down outside. By the time Noah reached the Stomper bay though there was no need of him. The decision not to launch any additional mechs was already made. Noah hadn't stuck around. As soon as he was told that the danger outside was over, he'd cleared out of the Stomper bay before those outside returned to the station.

When the alarm went up, Noah had been asleep in his bunk. Any other day he might have cursed it happening, wanting nothing more than to stay under the warm covers wrapped around him. Today though, the alarm saved him from his dreams or rather his nightmare. When the alarm woke him, Noah was covered in sweat, his covers wrapped far more tightly than usual about him as if he'd been twisting about inside during his sleep. Noah could sure believe that he had been. The nightmare was the strangest and most terrifying dream he'd ever had. Noah didn't have a clue where it had come from. His last thoughts before falling asleep weren't of the Deep Black. The patrol he'd finished with Riggs was just another day. Nothing really horrid or weird happened during it. Instead, Noah had been thinking about his father. His dad's exploits as a pilot were legendary. The old man had flown the deadly fighters of his time and was among the top contenders for enemy kills. Noah's father hadn't been happy that his son didn't want to fly but the invention of mech technology for hostile environments such as space and the ocean floor had sealed Noah's fate. All he'd wanted when he joined up was to pilot an armored suit like Pioneer 4's heavy Stompers. His father loved the roar of an engine and the feeling of pure speed, soaring through the clouds while Noah loved the hiss of a Stomper's tribarreled mini-gun needle blasters and the thud of his suit's footfalls. The two of them had rarely seen eye to eye when his father was alive. Noah regretted that, always wishing he could have made his dad see just how alike they really were despite their differences. Regardless of his thoughts and emotions, when Noah had laid down his head, all those things vanished, replaced by. . . horror. The nightmare that followed was unlike anything Noah had ever experienced.

As the nightmare began, Noah's dream self was on patrol inside his Stomper. The heavy mech thudded its way towards the wide, oceanic trench called the Deep Black. He was alone which wasn't all that odd but somehow struck him that way. The mouth of the trench was like an open wound in the ocean floor as his Stomper came to a halt and Noah found himself staring at it. There was no sign of the creatures that lived within its depths. Noah brought his Stomper to a halt at the edge of the trench. He looked down into the blackness which seemed to go on forever. Its intensity felt unnatural, chilling him to the bone despite the controlled environment inside his Stomper. Noah flinched as he saw something stirring in the black. It wasn't the creatures that the pilots of Pioneer 4 engaged in combat on nearly a daily basis. Whatever was moving in the dark was much larger than the creatures. Noah couldn't see what it was. The thing's shape was merged with the darkness. It was impossible to make out and his Stomper's sensors didn't register it all despite its massive size. Noah checked them to make sure they were working properly. They were. There was no sign of any issues with them though Noah couldn't understand why he could clearly see whatever was in the trench but they couldn't detect it at all. Was it real? Was he losing his mind? Had he suffered some kind of break down from the stresses of life on Pioneer 4 and the constant battles with the creatures from the Deep Black?

Noah shook his head to clear it, blinking his eyes. When he looked into the Deep Black again, there was nothing there but darkness. Whatever Noah thought he had seen down there was gone. He let out a sigh of relief. The whole experience was creepy as hell. Noah's Stomper half turned away from the Deep Black as he was about to head back towards Pioneer 4 and keep moving on his patrol of its perimeter. Before he could get the heavy mech truly moving something erupted from the trench. The thing was like a tidal wave of darkness, washing over his Stomper. Noah screamed inside the heavily armored mech as cold unlike anything he had ever felt hit him and that was the point where the alarm had woken him, sparing Noah from whatever would have happened next.

It was hard to explain even within his own mind but Noah knew in the dream he'd felt more than just cold when the darkness consumed his Stomper. It was like being embraced by pure evil. There was a keen and cruel intelligence within the darkness that touched his mind, threatening to take it over. In that moment, within the dream, Noah could feel that he was losing himself to it. He shuddered at that thought and thanked God he had been woken up before the thing made him its own.

Even now, the nightmare still haunted him no matter how much Noah tried to push his memories of it out of his mind. Noah sat on the edge of his bunk wringing his hands, wondering what the hell he was going to do about it. He needed desperately to talk to someone about it but didn't know who. Noah was ashamed atjust how freaked out by the nightmare he was. Soldiers weren't supposed to get scared like he was now, not from something that wasn't real anyway.

****

Dr. Jeffery was fuming from the news of the transport being destroyed. Word of what had happened with the Stompers and the attack by the creatures from the Deep Black had spread quickly throughout Pioneer 4. Dr. Lowery could understand what he was feeling. The man was going to be responsible for making up the difference in quota no matter who was found at fault. That meant a hell of a lot of work for her too but Dr. Lowery didn't care. As she was technically in a sort of training state in the eyes of the powers that be back home, whatever happened wasn't going to damage her career or standing like it was his. She watched Dr. Jeffery pacing about the room, cursing under his breath as she sat at Dr. Miller's station. She had the computer there powered up and open to the late doctor's research. Thankfully, Dr. Jeffery couldn't see what she was looking at from where he was. He'd dismissed Miller's work as a waste of time.

Dr. Lowery looked at the data on the screen in front of her. Though what Miller had been studying wasn't exactly her field, she did understand enough of the basics to realise the strangeness of the transmissions coming out of the Deep Black. Transmissions. . . that word didn't really fit what was happening. Not really. The seemingly random bursts of energy waves from the Deep Black had been graphed by Miller. His theory was apparently that the bursts of energy were either attempts of communication by some utterly inhuman thing within the trench or worse, and far more sinister. . . Miller's take on the energy suggested that he truly perceived it as a direct threat to the

Pioneer 4 station. She'd skimmed his notes and either Miller had been as insane as Dr. Jeffery and some of the other personnel claimed he was or the man was a full out genius who had stumbled onto something horrible. Her fingers clicked away on the keyboard, pulling up current readings of the energy from the Deep Black. They pulsated on the screen as she watched them. Were they growing stronger? It sure looked like it.

According to Dr. Miller's notes, he believed that the strange energy waves were capable of penetrating the armor and shielding of Pioneer 4. With further investigation, he'd proven, at least to himself, that those waves were affecting certain areas of the human brain and thus influencing those within the station. Dr. Miller made several attempts at finding a means to block the waves. . . all of which had failed. It appeared Miller had given up approaching the problem from that direction and opted instead to delve deeper into how the energy might be affecting the crew. There, he looked to have been having some success but it was also the point where his notes had simply stopped. Dr. Lowery assumed that those were the last Dr. Miller made before being killed.

"Lowery!" Dr. Jeffery yelled at her, suddenly stopping his pacing. The gaze of his angry eyes fell upon her. "What the Hell are you doing over there?"

Sucking in a startled breath, Dr. Lowery jerked upright in her seat though she didn't answer him. Dr. Lowery was well aware of how Dr. Jeffery felt about Miller's work.

"I asked you a question," Dr. Jeffery growled.

"I was just. . ." Dr. Lowery started but was unable to finish. She was interrupted, betrayed, by the computer. The harsh screech of a warning blared out from it as the energy readings from the Deep Black spiked, increasing a hundred fold.

"What the hell?" Dr. Lowery exclaimed in pure shock as Dr. Jeffery lunged towards her.

"What is that?" he demanded, spittle flying from his lips.

"It's. . ." Dr. Lowery got out before Dr. Jeffery shoved her roughly away from the computer.

"This is Miller's fragging detection program, isn't it?" Dr. Jeffery raged.

"The energy coming from the Deep Black . . ." Dr. Lowery told him. "It's gone off the scale!"

Dr. Jeffery slammed a fist down onto the computer's keyboard, breaking several of its keys. The screen above the keyboard went black as his other hand snaked around behind it, ripping the power cable there loose.

"What are you doing?" Dr. Lowery challenged him, her fear turning into anger.

"We've just been put farther behind the corporate production timetable than I have ever been before, God only knows how much money was lost with the destruction of that transport, and you. . .you're messing around with Miller's crap again?" Dr. Jeffery shot back at her. "I should have the colonel bring you up on charges!"

"Charges? What for? I'm doing my damn job, Jeffery!" Dr. Lowery shouted. "That's more than can be said about you!"

"Our job. . .Our job is to produce the extract from those creatures, Lowery, and ensure that the flow of it never stops. That's what our job is!" Dr. Jeffery turned his back to the black screen of the computer and took a step towards her.

Dr. Lowery didn't so much as flinch. She was ready for him now. There wasn't a shred of fear left in her knowing full well that, despite what he was saying, their job went beyond just the harvesting of the extract.

"We were assigned here to study the Deep Black too," Dr. Lowery argued, holding her ground. "And no matter what you thought of Miller, you can't deny that he was onto something after seeing readings like the ones we just did."

"That's bull!" Dr. Jeffery threw his hands up in frustration. "And you know it! That energy coming out of the Deep Black is nothing to be concerned about. Losing an entire damned transport of extract. . . that. . . that is dangerous! Do you know what the powers that be back home will do to us if we don't make this right by yesterday?"

"That doesn't matter right now. They can't touch us down here! That energy though, it can and is!" Dr. Lowery pointed out. Then she caught herself, realizing just how insane both she and Dr. Jeffery were being. Sure, things were tense, there were lots of stressors, but even so, what they were doing was over the top. Dr. Lowery's gaze had sunk downward as her thoughts became clearer. She looked up at Dr. Jeffery knowing she had to try to get him to calm down too. As she did, a clenched fist slammed into her jaw. She stumbled sideways, thudding into the wall before being able to catch herself.

Dr. Lowery tasted blood. She spat and rose up as Dr. Jeffery came at her again. Lowery was no prize fighter but she had taken self-defense classes. Those reflexes kicked in now saving her from another injury. Her right arm shot up, making contact with Dr. Jeffery's, knocking aside the blow intended for her head. Moving with grace and speed Dr. Lowery didn't fully know she was capable of, her left hand shot forward, striking Dr. Jeffery in the center of his throat. A pained noise escaped him as he reeled backwards. Dr. Lowery followed through with a kick to his chest that knocked him to the floor. He landed on his back with a loud thud, gasping for breath.

Standing over him, Dr. Lowery had slipped into an instinctive defensive stance. Surprised by her own actions, Dr. Lowery was grinning like an awestruck fool. She looked down at him to see Dr. Jeffery rubbing his throat. There was something chilling in the expression he wore as his head tilted to meet her gaze. Something was off with his eyes.

"Angela Lowery," Dr. Jeffery spoke with a voice that wasn't his. Hell, it didn't even sound human. His voice was cold, piercing, and deeper than it had any right to be.

Dr. Lowery took a step backwards away from him as he rose up from the floor. Her fists clenched even tighter. A sort of primal fear gripped Dr. Lowery and beads of sweat formed on her skin. Though it made no rational sense at all, something inside of her told Dr. Lowery that it wasn't Dr. Jeffery who was speaking to her anymore.

Dr. Jeffery's throat was bruised from her blow but he showed no sign of feeling pain from it anymore. His voice boomed with an almost supernatural strength as he spoke again. "Your predecessor stumbled onto my voice as well. Unfortunately for him, Miller refused to let me in and listen to it though. What will your choice be I wonder, Dr. Lowery?"

She didn't know how to respond. Truth be told, Dr. Lowery didn't really understand what he was asking. Hell, she couldn't even believe what was clearly happening right before her own eyes. Something had taken Dr. Jeffery over.

"Don't worry," Dr. Jeffery grinned wickedly as he advanced towards her, "You don't have to decide now."

"Stay the hell away from me, Doctor, or I'll. . . " Dr. Lowery warned.

"Or you'll what?" the thing that had once been Dr. Jeffery cackled.

"Or I'll put you right back down on your arse again," Dr. Lowery said, trying to sound braver and tougher than she felt.

Dr. Jeffery laughed. "I'd like to see that," he thumped his hands against his chest. "This weakling wouldn't have stood a chance against you but I think you're smart enough to realize that he's not here anymore."

"What. . .?" Dr. Lowery got out before Dr. Jeffery lunged at her.

She snapped out a kick meant to meet and stop his rushing form but Dr. Jeffery jerked to the right fast enough to escape its impact. He kept coming forward though, plowing into her so hard that the breath was knocked from Dr. Lowery's lungs. She was flung over backwards onto the floor with him coming down on top of her. Dr. Jeffery's hands caught her wrists, pinning her own to the floor behind her head. His head cocked at an angle like an animal studying its prey above her.

"Oh yes, Angela," Dr. Jeffery smiled, "We're going to have so much fun."

****

Becca sat with her hands bound by handcuffs that were so tight they bruised her wrists. The chair she was in was far from comfortable and positioned in the center of the cell Becca had been brought to. Colonel Hendricks, Steward, and Duffman all stood around her. Steward stood like a stone sentry at the cell's door, Duffman leaned against the wall that she was facing, while the colonel paced the cell floor, hands clasped rigidly behind her back. Becca knew she'd screwed up, knew the amount of trouble that would be waiting on her with the powers that be back home. Still, it was the colonel that scared her the most. Hendricks, at least to her, had grown more and more aggressive and vindictive since all the crap with Marshal Hershey. God only knew what the colonel had planned for her down here where there was no one to see or hear what happened. All Becca knew for sure was that it was likely going to hurt like hell.

Colonel Hendricks abruptly stopped her pacing directly in front of Becca, spinning about sharply on her heel so they faced one another head on. "Do you have any idea just how badly you've screwed us all over, pilot?"

"Yes ma'am," Becca said, keeping her voice flat and calm, forcing herself to show what respect she could manage for her C.O.

"And what do you have to say for yourself?" Colonel Hendricks snarled.

"It was an accident, ma'am," Becca lied. She didn't have a fragging clue what happened to her out there in the deep, inside her Stomper. It was as if something had taken her over and used her as if she were nothing more than a puppet to do its will. Becca sure wasn't about to try and explain that to Colonel Hendricks. She couldn't even explain it to herself.

Colonel Hendricks glared intently at Becca. "I'm not sure locking you up in here is enough of a punishment for what you've done. What do you boys think?"

Duffman snorted. "Not nearly enough."

Steward didn't respond to the colonel's question. He just continued standing at the cell's door, arms crossed over his chest. But then a noise from somewhere outside of the cell drew all of their attention towards it. Colonel Hendricks looked more angry than concerned about whatever it was. Becca hoped it was the new marshal. She figured he was likely the only person in Pioneer 4 who had the power to stop the colonel from carrying out her own brand of justice.

It wasn't Marshal McShane that Steward stepped aside to allow entrance to the cell though. It was Dr. Foxx, the station's counselor, who came rushing in.

"Colonel!" Dr. Foxx snapped. "Exactly what is going on in here?"

"Doctor, not that it's any of your business, but I am preparing to interrogate this prisoner about what happened to the transport."

"What happened?" Dr. Foxx repeated. "It was destroyed, Colonel. Shot to bits. I'd say that's obvious. There's even video footage of it happening. So I will ask again, Colonel, what are you doing in here? Locking Becca away in here is well within your authority but this. . .what is this anyway? Perhaps a means in which you can lash out for the loss you've suffered."

Colonel Hendricks gave a disgusted snort. "Steward, escort Dr. Foxx out of the brig."

Steward reached for Dr. Foxx but she slapped the hand he was about to place on her shoulder away. "Keep your hands off of me, soldier. I'm not going anywhere until I know that Becca's not going to be hurt."

Becca was impressed by Dr. Foxx's courage. It took a hell of a lot to stand up to three armed soldiers especially when one of them was the station's C.O. and known to have a violent streak.

Steward awkwardly stood looking as if he

didn't know what to do. Becca knew he wasn't the complete nut job that Colonel Hendricks could be. He wasn't as cold and hardened as Duffman either. There was still something inside of him capable of feeling mercy or at least some tiny shred of compassion.

"Oh frag this," Colonel Hendricks suddenly barked. She drew the pistol holstered on her hip with such speed that none of them even realized it was happening until it was too late. The pistol cracked and Dr. Foxx's head snapped back atop her neck. The bullet Colonel Hendricks fired had punched a hole in the doctor's forehead, killing Foxx instantly.

Steward jerked away from Dr. Foxx's collapsing corpse, a look of mixed shock and terror on his face. Colonel Hendricks' pistol cracked again. Steward lurched forward, staggering a few feet towards the Colonel before stopping. His eyes fell to take in the growing stain of red that was blossoming on his shirt. Then without being able to get out a single word, Steward toppled to the floor. Becca heard the crunch of breaking bone as his nose broke beneath the weight of his body.

"Colonel!" Duffman shouted, his cold and aloof demeanor gone, replaced by something else. Whether that something else was the drive of self-preservation or some sense of military discipline that told the big man what was happening was wrong, Becca didn't know. In the end, it didn't matter.

Colonel Hendricks put a round into Duffman's left knee, shattering it. The wounded leg gave way under him and Duffman fell to the cell's floor. He managed to draw his sidearm on the way down though. It came up towards the colonel but before he could use it, another round from her struck his gun hand. Duffman's gun was flung out of his grasp by the bullet's impact. It bounced across the cell, out of his reach.

"Ah ah," Colonel Hendricks cautioned Duffman. "That'll be quite enough from you unless you want to join Steward in Hell."

Unable to stop herself, Becca leaned forward in her chair, hands still bound, and vomited. It splattered between her feet. The sight of Dr. Foxx's mangled forehead and the brain matter leaking out was too much for her. It was one thing to watch other soldiers or monsters die but entirely different to see such a normally timid and soft woman die so unexpectedly in such a violent manner.

"Weak," Colonel Hendricks chuckled. "That's what you are, Becca. You know that, don't you?"

"Colonel," Duffman pleaded from where he lay clutching his shot up hand in a pool of his own blood.

"Shut up, Duffman," Colonel Hendricks growled. "I don't need to hear your whimpering too. Keep it up and you'll regret it. Me too honestly as I have other plans for you."

Becca looked up in the direction of Colonel Hendricks' voice. A chill ran through her and Becca shuddered. The colonel's eyes were glowing. Becca blinked, staring at Hendricks in disbelief.

"You look surprised to see me again, Becca?" Colonel Hendrick's lips parted in a wide smile beneath her brightly glowing yellow eyes. "I'd have thought you would have recognized my voice already."

Swallowing hard, Becca knew who was speaking to her. It wasn't Colonel Hendricks at all. It was the thing that had been inside her head. The thing that had forced her to fire into the transport and blow it apart. It was inside the colonel now.

Colonel Hendricks shifted her pistol to her left hand. Walking up to Becca, she reached out with the fingers of her right to wipe away the spots of vomit on the restrained pilot's lips.

"My dear little Becca," Colonel Hendricks purred. "Do you know what time it is?"

Becca attempted to shake her head weakly but Hendricks' hand prevented her from doing so.

"That's okay," Colonel Hendricks whispered gently. "That's okay. You're only human after all."

"What. . .what time is it?" Becca managed to

get the words out through her partly held closed mouth.

"It's time for the fun to truly start," Colonel Hendricks cackled.

"Leave her alone!" Duffman yelled, the fingers of his good hand clutched tight around his leg above the remnants of his shattered knee.

The foul grin Colonel Hendricks wore only grew wider. Holstering her pistol, she leaned down to reach into her right boot. From it, she pulled out a small but gleamingly sharp combat knife and started walking towards Duffman.

****

Wrinkler was sitting at the controls of the Stomper bay when Noah found him. The new tech hadn't answered when Noah had called out his name so he'd gone looking for him.

"What can I do for you, pilot?" Wrinkler asked as Noah entered the control room to stand behind where he sat.

"There's not a patrol out there right now, Wrinkler," Noah said flatly. "The colonel hasn't ordered anyone back out so I am here to volunteer."

"I suspect the colonel's been busy," Wrinkler huffed.

"What's that supposed to mean?" Noah said, his tone more defensive than he meant it to be.

"Colonel Hendricks sure isn't what I thought

she'd be," Wrinkler answered, turning around in his chair to look at Noah.

Noah stared at the Stomper tech waiting for him to explain what he'd just said a bit better.

"I think you know what I mean," Wrinkler finally said.

Noah sighed. He supposed the tech was right. Colonel Hendricks wasn't exactly a stellar role model as an officer.

"I guess so," Noah admitted. "Regardless, someone should be out there in case those creatures come back."

"I may have just arrived here recently but I know that this base was built to withstand those things with or without Stompers adding their firepower to its automated defenses," Wrinkler said. "And you know that I can't let you go out there alone without an order from the colonel."

"I'd argue these are some pretty exceptional circumstances we're dealing with right now, Wrinkler," Noah pressed him.

Wrinkler shrugged. "My hands are bound by protocol. You going out there alone without orders ain't happening on my watch, Noah. I'm sorry."

"There's nothing I can do to change your mind?" Noah asked.

"Find another pilot to go with you and we'll talk," Wrinkler offered. "Until then. . ."

"Copy that," Noah reluctantly agreed. "You get two Stompers ready, Wrinkler, and I'll be back before you know it."

"Sure thing," Wrinkler nodded and watched Noah hurry out of the Stomper Bay control room.

Wrinkler shook his head. Noah and he were close to the same age but that was about all they had in common. Noah was a strapping specimen of what a young soldier was expected to be. He was well muscled unlike Wrinkler who was lean and some might even label scrawny. Noah was full of bravado too. Wrinkler didn't think of himself as a coward but Noah. . .he was trying to rush outside, maybe get himself killed, just to do his duty. That's what it really was, not some compassionate need to protect those within the walls of Pioneer 4. Wrinkler could see that much from just looking at him. Noah's drive came from a need for excitement, glory, and personal honor. Wrinkler cared about performing his duty well too and knew if it came down to it, he would surrender his life as well but rushing to do it like Noah appeared to be. . . nope. That was just fragged up to him.

Returning his attention to the monitor screen he'd been looking at before Noah came bursting in, Wrinkler stretched, his back arcing in his chair, hands thrust upwards above his head, fingers interlocked. Several of his joints popped. Easing his arms back down, Wrinkler reached to pick up the mug of cold, black coffee that sat on the edge of the console in front of him.

The control room had access to the feeds of Pioneer 4's external cameras. On the monitor, Wrinkler had the best possible view of the trench called The Deep Black called up. He would never be leaving the station like Noah and the other pilots. This was the closest he was ever going to be to it. The Deep Black fascinated Wrinkler. Some might look at it and see nothing more than just another oceanic trench. Without knowing what was within its depths, Wrinkler might have too. He did know though. At least he knew some. Wrinkler knew about the creatures and the extract that could prolong human life. Wrinkler wondered what else lay within the deep, dark waters below the mouth of the trench.

He chugged what was left of his coffee and returned the mug to the edge of the console, his eyes never leaving the image of the Deep Black on the screen. Squinting, Wrinkler focused his gaze on a single, small section of the trench's darkness. There was something there in that blackness, Wrinkler knew it. As if in answer to the intensity of his scrutiny, a glimmer of light flashed there.

"What the. . . ?" Wrinkler snapped upright in his chair. Had he been dozing off and dreamed what he'd just seen? Was he losing his mind from the stress of everything that was going on inside the station? There was no way what he'd just seen should have been possible. There was nothing within the trench that could have produced a flash like the one he'd seen. Before his reeling mind could even finish coming to terms with the first flash, another happened and then another.

Wrinkler leaned forward, fingers dancing over the keys of the controls. He ran a quick diagnostic on the camera and the other systems he was using to watch the Deep Black. Everything came up green. There were no signs of any issues with the station's cameras, sensors, or the computer system itself.

The light was pulsating rapidly now. Wrinkler stared at it, watching its flickers closely. Then suddenly he realized there was a pattern to its flashing. The damn thing was giving him a message in fragging morse code.

Leaping out of his chair, Wrinkler rushed about searching for a pen and something to write on. As soon as they were in hand, he returned to his seat in front of the console and began jotting down the message that was somehow inexplicably and insanely being sent to him. When the pattern began to repeat, Wrinkler stopped scrawling it down on the paper. His eyes slowly scanned over the words he had written down.

They read "Thank you for letting me in."

In that exact instant, Wrinkler felt as if

someone had plunged a flaming hot nail into his mind. He screamed, thrashing about in his chair and out of it onto the control room floor. Wrinkler's legs kicked wildly as his hands clenched into fists so tightly that his fingernails pressed into their flesh deep enough to draw blood. Inwardly, everything that was Wrinkler struggled against the thing that was now within him. It threatened to consume all of what he was, memories, hopes, dreams, fears. . . there would be nothing left when it was done. The thing's being was partly open to him and Wrinkler glimpsed its plans.

Vomit poured from Wrinkler's mouth. It wasn't coughed up or hurled out but rather slowly forced up as if simply sliding out of him. He was able to unclench his hands. Pressing them flat onto the floor, Wrinkler heaved himself up to his feet. His balance was off. It was hard to stay on his feet. Wrinkler grabbed the edge of the Stomper Bay's control console. He and the thing inside of him had very different plans for what needed to happen in the span of the next few moments. Wrinkler knew that there was more than just his own fate at stake. With every fiber of his being Wrinkler wanted to destroy the controls. His eyes darted about, searching the control room for something he could use to smash the console. Wrinkler didn't have the strength or steadiness to pick up the chair he'd been sitting in and be able to keep up the struggle inside of himself too.

Then Wrinkler screamed again. It rang out like the dying howl of a hurting animal. He collapsed onto his knees in front of the console. Only the fingers of his hand clawing out to grab its edge once more kept him from going completely down. His body shuddered and spasmed. His head shot up as a burst of bright red blood exploded outward from between his vomit coated lips. The blood splattered over the keys of the console. Then Wrinkler went suddenly still. His eyes closed. When they opened, a yellow glow shined out from them.

****

Marshal Robert McShane was on his way to the Brig but had decided to stop and check in on Dr. Lowery, figuring she might be able to give him some more insight into all the insanity happening with the Pioneer 4 station. He knew she was supposed to be in the main lab. As its door hissed open before him, McShane's eyes went wide at what he saw. Dr. Lowery was on the floor with Dr. Jeffery on top of her, pinning her down, as she fought to break free. McShane's mind didn't even attempt to make sense of what he saw. He lunged forward, his hands grabbing the backside of Dr. Jeffery's lab coat. McShane flung the man away from Dr. Lowery.

Dr. Jeffery thudded onto the floor a few feet

away from McShane but didn't stay down. The man recovered far faster than he would have thought possible. McShane noticed the yellow glow of his eyes as Dr. Jeffery scrambled back onto his feet and sprang at him like a feral animal. Standing his ground, McShane's right fist met the jaw of the snarling doctor. The impact sent a mouthful of blood and several teeth flying from Jeffery's mouth. Still, it didn't stop Jeffery. He kept coming, hands clawing at McShane.

Keeping his cool, McShane used Jeffery's own momentum against him, slamming the doctor into the metal wall of the lab. He followed up with a quick series of blows to the doctor's midsection. They seemed to have almost no effect on the snarling wild man as Dr. Jeffery's fingernails tried to dig into McShane's shoulders but were unable to pierce the thick material of his jacket.

Afraid to release Dr. Jeffery, McShane switched tactics. He slammed his head forward into the doctor's which was enough to stun Jeffery, even in his wigged out state. McShane used the moment to sling Jeffery around again, hurling him onto the floor once more. As Dr. Jeffery slid across the lab floor, McShane yanked his sidearm free of the holster on his hip.

"Stay the frag down!" Marshal McShane warned as Dr. Jeffery moved to get up.

When he saw that the doctor wasn't going to listen to him, McShane fired two carefully aimed shots in rapid succession. They slammed into Dr. Jeffery's kneecaps. Blood and fragments of bone exploded out of them. McShane hated to do it but didn't figure there was any other choice. He had to keep the doctor on the floor. The man was clearly, utterly out of his head and deadly dangerous. It was like Dr. Jeffery was on some kind of aggression inducing drug.

Dr. Jeffery screeched in pain as his knee joints were blown apart beneath his skin. Still not wanting to take any chances, McShane rushed over to him and gave the doctor a rough kick to the forehead. That did the trick, knocking Dr. Jeffery unconscious.

"Marshal!" Dr. Lowery shouted from behind him. McShane spun about to see her getting up from the floor of the lab. Once she was on her feet, her hands worked at smoothing out the white cloth of the lab coat she wore. "Thank God you showed up. He was about to kill me."

"What in the devil happened to him?" McShane asked.

"I'm not sure you would believe me if I told you," Dr. Lowery said.

"Try me," McShane told her.

"I am sure you're aware that my predecessor, Dr. Milner, was studying the energy pulses that are coming out of the Deep Black. . ." Dr.

Lowery frowned.

"Are you saying that Marshal Hershey was right?" McShane asked.

"You know about. . ." Dr. Lowery stammered though he couldn't tell if her wavering voice was from what she had just been through or shock at him knowing.

"I read through his files," McShane explained. "The man was convinced that there was something inside the Deep Black that was affecting the personnel of this station."

"He was right," Dr. Lowery frowned, nodding her head. "The proof of it is lying at your feet."

Marshal McShane glanced down at Dr. Jeffery as Dr. Lowery continued.

"The energy coming out of that trench is doing a hell of a lot more than just messing with us, Marshal," Dr. Lowery's eyes were wide with fear. "I believe that whatever is producing the energy is not only alive but intelligent."

"That makes sense," Marshal McShane agreed.

"The thing in the trench. . .I don't know why but I think it wants us all dead," Dr. Lowery told him.

"Does it matter?" McShane challenged her. "I figure the real question is how do we stop it? Clearly the shielding on the station hasn't done crap in keeping the energy out."

"I. . .I'm not sure that we can stop it," Dr.

Lowery admitted.

"I'm going to need you to do better than that, Doctor," McShane said.

"You can stop those under the thing's influence. That's something, right?" Dr. Lowery shrugged. "And some of us. . . it's not going to be able to influence or take over. Some of us are going to have biological issues with our brain chemistry or simply just too strong of wills for the thing to overcome."

"Good to know," McShane nodded. "So if it wants us all dead, why does it seem like this thing has been just toying with us instead of going all out already?"

Dr. Lowery shrugged. "Could be it was building up its strength, getting a feel for just how far and who it could affect, before making a final push or the thing could just like to play with its prey like a cat might."

"I'm inclined to think the former is more likely," McShane commented and then gently kicked Dr. Jeffery's unconscious body. "And based how open it was with this guy, I'd say the thing is ready to make whatever move it has been planning."

****

"Frag it, Noah," Riggs grumbled. "Colonel Hendricks has Becca locked up in the brig doing God only knows what to her and you want me to just forget it?"

Riggs was sitting on the edge of his bunk. He had been waiting on Marshal McShane to show up and let him know that Becca was at the very least safe from the colonel's fury. When Noah came bursting in, his disappointment at seeing it was just Noah had been clear on his face. Of course that hadn't stopped the kid from trying to get what he wanted though. The two of them were still arguing about it.

Noah shook his head. "Sarge, there's no one out there watching the trench. No one. And we were just attacked, for frag's sake."

"This station has been attacked before, Noah," Riggs countered, "And by much bigger numbers than what was out there today. Besides, this station has its own defenses."

"Automated ones, sure, but do you really want to trust all our lives to some programmed A.I.?" Noah argued. "Having some Stompers out there, ready to engage the creatures if they hit us again, could make all the difference in the world."

"I like your passion, kid, but. . ." Riggs sighed.

"Look," Noah slammed a fist into the wall of Riggs' quarters. "You can't do anything to help Becca by just sitting there. Besides, you said Marshal McShane was dealing with the colonel anyway. I've met the guy. Trust me, he won't let Colonel Hendricks overstep her authority or do anything that would really hurt Becca. If you come with me, you might be saving them both, everyone, and you know it, sir."

"What makes you think those things will even hit us again anytime soon, Noah?" Riggs asked. "They don't normally come running right back after we've handed them their butts on a platter like we did today, kid."

Noah gritted his teeth in frustration. "I don't know how to explain it, sir. I just have a feeling that they're coming back."

"A feeling?" Riggs smirked.

"Please, Sergeant," Noah begged him. "That new Stomper tech, Wrinkler, he's on duty in the bay and won't let me take a suit out without another pilot going on patrol with me."

That got Riggs' attention.

"What?" Riggs stood up. "He doesn't have that kind of authority."

"Well Wrinkler sure acted like he did," Noah said.

Riggs grunted, admitting to himself that Noah might be right about what the newbie, Wrinkler, could and couldn't do under the actual regulations. "Maybe, but he sure as hell can't pull that crap on me, kid."

"Does that mean you'll go with me?" Noah gasped.

"I didn't say that," Riggs shook his head. "What I will do though is go with you to the Bay and make sure you get out there seeing as how you're so convinced those things might already be on their way back."

"That's good enough for me!" Noah exclaimed. "Thank you, Sergeant Riggs."

Riggs pulled on his jacket, heading for the door of his quarters. "Come on, kid. Let's get this over with."

Noah followed in his wake like an excited puppy.

The corridors between Riggs' quarters and the Stomper Bay were empty of other personnel. That wasn't really unusual for this time of day but even so it made Riggs wonder if Noah's feeling of dread was contagious.

When they entered the Stomper Bay, it was just as deserted.

"Wrinkler!" Riggs shouted, not seeing the tech around.

When no answer came, Noah said, "Last time I saw him, Wrinkler was up in the control room."

"Then I guess that's where we're headed." Riggs stomped towards the small set of steps leading up to the sealed room where Noah last saw Wrinkler.

"Riggs!" Noah called after him.

The sergeant stopped and turned around. "What?"

"I got a bad feeling about this, man," Noah frowned.

"Frag me, kid! What don't you have a freaking feeling about?" Riggs huffed.

Noah didn't answer.

"We still doing this or what?" Riggs barked at the young pilot.

"Yes sir," Noah nodded and hurried to catch up.

The control room wasn't locked. It never was. There was no need for that kind of security in a place like Pioneer 4 where everyone was supposedly on the same team. The door slid open to allow them entrance. Riggs and Noah went in side by side. Neither one of them was prepared for what was waiting for them in the darkness. Wrinkler sprang at them like a madman. His right hand clutched something that looked like a ceramic shard from a shattered coffee mug. That hand was bloody, the shard seeming to be cutting into his own palm. The newbie tech's lips were parted in a snarl. Worst of all, his eyes were glowing a sickening shade of yellow that made him look completely inhuman. Only Riggs' battle-hardened reflexes saved him from getting the shard of ceramic stabbed into the side of his neck.

Riggs parried Wrinkler's attack, swinging up an arm to knock away the hand clutching the shard. Wrinkler still slammed into the sergeant though. The tech didn't have the strength or weight even with his momentum to really move Riggs. Grunting, Riggs held his ground, grabbing Wrinkler's right arm. His fingers closed around it tightly, jerking it up enough to jar Wrinkler's makeshift weapon from his grasp. In a normal fight, Riggs would have likely won in that moment, having disarmed Wrinkler and being in a position to immobilize him by pinning the tech with a bear hug by his thickly muscled arms. This fight was anything but normal though. Wrinkler was truly like a wild animal. The tech shoved his head forward. Riggs screamed as Wrinkler's teeth bit into the flesh of his cheek. A large chunk of it was torn away as Wrinkler reared his head back.

Noah stood watching the fight, held in place by utter shock and disbelief.

"Help me, damn it!" Riggs yelled.

The sergeant's gruff voice snapped Noah into action. He rushed forward, taking hold of the tech from behind. Noah flung Wrinkler away from Riggs and moved quickly to take him out of action. He bashed a fist into Wrinkler's forehead, snapping his head back atop his neck. The blow slowed Wrinkler but didn't stop him. Noah retreated as Wrinkler clawed at him, drawing blood where the tech's fingernails met the exposed flesh of the sides of his neck. Desperate to regain the initiative and control of their struggle, Noah rammed a knee up into Wrinkler's groin. With a pained grunt, Wrinkler went down, collapsing onto his knees in front of him. Noah clasped his fists together and swung them in an arc downward onto the top of Wrinkler's head with a loud thump. Glowing yellow eyes rolled up in their sockets, as Wrinker was knocked unconscious.

"Fragging bastard!" Noah shouted, kicking Wrinkler several more times before Riggs moved to stop him.

"That's enough, kid," Riggs ordered. "He's out already."

Noah stopped, slowly turning his head to look at Riggs. "What the hell is wrong with him?"

"You got me," Riggs shrugged. "I think we've got bigger things to worry about though."

"What. . .?" Noah stammered but Riggs was already moving towards the control room's main console where something appeared to be counting down.

"He's got the bay doors opening," Riggs shouted. "Several other airlocks all around the station too!"

"Why the hell would he do that?" Noah demanded.

"You saw him, right?" Riggs snapped. "That guy was gone!"

"Can we stop. . .?" Noah started.

"Not a chance in hell," Riggs shook his head. "We need to get out of here! When the bay doors open, this entire section of the station will be flooded in seconds."

"What about him?" Noah asked, gesturing at Wrinkler, as Riggs was already heading for the control room's door.

"Leave him!" Riggs growled. "He did this. The bastard deserves what he's about to get."

Riggs and Noah raced out of the control room. Jumping the steps to the floor of the bay, Riggs landed, his boots thudding onto the metal beneath them. Noah was right on his heels. Sprinting for the closest exit, Riggs glanced back across the bay to see the huge exterior doors opening. As they parted, with their safety mechanisms disabled, water came exploding into the bay, spraying out from between them like lava from an erupting volcano.

Making it into the corridor they had been heading for, Riggs stopped just inside its entrance at the control panel there. Waves of water were already rushing past them, almost up to their knees, making it hard to keep their footing. Riggs' fingers tapped furiously at the panel's keys, inputting his authorization codes. He thanked God as his code worked. The alarm klaxons Wrinkler had disabled began to blare and the bulkhead doors that were designed to seal the Stomper bay in case of a breach slammed into place cutting off the stream of water pouring into the corridor with them.

"That was fragging close!" Noah yelped.

"We ain't out of the woods yet, kid," Riggs warned. "I was only able to seal the bay. The other places that lunatic opened up. . . God only knows what's going on with them."

Noah stared at Riggs, his eyes wide.

"Come on!" Riggs barked. "We gotta let the others know what's going on!"

****

McShane sprinted through the corridors of Pioneer 4 towards the station's brig. He skidded to a halt as alarm klaxons began to blare. "What the Hell?" he muttered. As the station's new marshal, McShane hadn't been around long enough to know if there were various kinds of alarm klaxons that signaled different things. What he did know was that whatever was going on. . . it had to be bad. Really bad. From the intensity of the klaxons, he guessed either the station had been breached or boarded or both. McShane cursed, hoping that there was someone else who could deal with whatever had set off the klaxons. Right now, his hands were full. He'd cuffed Dr. Jeffery up in the lab but still didn't like leaving Dr. Lowery alone with . . . whatever the man had become. His gut told him that whatever took over Jeffery was also messing with Colonel Hendricks. It would explain her actions of late and why she didn't exactly match up with the image of the competent leader the woman's file painted Hendricks as being. And if his hunch was right then Becca, the Stomper pilot the colonel had taken into custody, could be in some serious trouble. Hell, the pilot could be dead already but McShane had to try to save her. It was his fragging job.

Ignoring the continuing blare of the klaxons, Marshal McShane got moving again. He was almost to the brig. As he ran, McShane slid the pistol on his hip free of its holster. McShane told himself it was just a precaution, that he wouldn't really need to use it. He reached the door to the brig. It was locked and McShane was forced to use his personal codes to override it.

The door to the brig slid open. The first thing McShane saw was the blood. . .splattered everywhere. It spotted the walls and slicked the floor. His eyes scanned the room. The pilot he'd come to save was still alive. Becca was bound to the chair she sat in, a pool of vomit on the floor between her legs. There was a look of sheer horror on her face that chilled McShane to his core.

A woman he hadn't met yet but knew to be the station's counselor, Dr. Foxx, lay not far from the entrance where he stood. She was face down on her stomach. The white of bone could be seen where a round fired at close range had punched through and exited. Brain matter clumped in her hair around the wound. There was the corpse of a soldier too. He had the same sort of exit wound in his back, opposite the center of his chest. A single shot through the heart had set his soul free.

A sharp cackle of sick glee drew McShane's attention. He looked towards the other side of the room to see Colonel Hendricks kneeling next to the twitching form of a soldier. In her hand was a combat knife as she smiled at him. The hand that held the knife was drenched in blood that wasn't her own. Red soaked most of her uniform as well. The poor bastard she'd been cutting on was somehow alive despite the damage Hendricks had done to him. McShane could see that Hendricks had skinned the man's cheeks, revealing the muscle under where his flesh had been. His lips were missing. Several of his teeth were broken and looked as if she'd hammered his mouth more than once with the pommel of her knife. One of his eyes was nothing more than an empty socket, ragged meat surrounding it and dangling bits of sinew leaking from its depths. The mutilations weren't contained to the soldier's face. Colonel Hendricks appeared to have been working on him for a while. His pants were down to his knees, white underwear red with seeping blood. It was obvious that Colonel Hendricks had relieved the soldier of his manhood as well as cut deep grooves up along the lengths of his thighs. His gaze wrenched up and away from the dying soldier towards Colonel Hendricks as she spoke.

"Welcome to the brig, Marshal," she chuckled. "I was beginning to wonder if you'd make it."

Colonel Hendricks ended the life of the soldier, finishing him by flipping her knife around in her hand and plunging its blade straight into his heart. The mutilated soldier's body jerked, back arcing up from the floor, and then fell back, utterly still. McShane heard the man suck in his final pained breath before death claimed him.

"Drop the fragging knife, Colonel," Marshal McShane snapped, bringing up his pistol so that its barrel was aimed at her head.

"I don't think so," Colonel Hendricks chuckled, getting to her feet, and giving the corpse of the soldier at her feet a last glance before meeting his eyes with her own.

McShane's pistol boomed. The round it fired ripped through the center of the colonel's throat, sending her staggering backwards. Her knife fell from her hand, clattering onto the metal below it, as he fired twice more. Both shots thudded into Colonel Hendricks' chest, knocking her from her feet.

"Thank God," McShane heard Becca cry out. "It's over."

McShane looked around at the pilot where she sat bound in the center of the room and shook his head. "No, it's not."

"What the hell is that supposed to mean?" Becca asked, the relief that seemed to have washed over her turning back to fear.

"I'm going to untie you," McShane told her, walking behind her where he could get at her bounds. "Don't do anything stupid, okay? I'm here to help."

"I won't," Becca promised. "I know who you are."

McShane got her loose and helped Becca to her feet. She was a bit unsteady so McShane reached out to brace her until Becca found her balance.

"Thanks," Becca said. "You got here just in time to save me. I was up next as soon as she was finished with him."

She nodded at the mutilated corpse.

Becca was holding up amazingly well for everything she'd just been through and witnessed.

"I always knew she was a bit off but this. . ." Becca shook her head.

"It wasn't all her," McShane told her.

"Yeah. It was. I just watched it all while I was bound to that chair," Becca argued.

"Not what I meant. She wasn't entirely herself anymore. There was more to what happened in here than just Hendricks losing it," McShane explained.

Becca stared at him. "Come again."

"There's something out there. . .in the Deep Black," McShane told her. "It's the same thing that drove Marshal Hershey insane. I don't know what it is but Dr. Lowery has proof that the thing affecting everyone on this station to some degree, is trying to make us turn on each other."

"Then I'm not crazy," Becca sounded relieved.

It was McShane's turn to stare at her.

"Out there, during the attack, something forced its way into my head, my mind," Becca admitted. "I felt it. Whatever it was, it was like pure violent evil. I really thought I was losing my mind."

"You weren't," McShane managed a smile. "Not in the way you just meant anyway. That thing very well could have just used you as a tool to blow up that transport. Maybe it knew how much doing that would stir up things even more on this station."

"When it was in my head. . . I got the impression it was smart as hell and old, really fragging old," Becca said. "It won't be easy to stop. I mean how do we even. . ?"

"No fragging clue," McShane grunted. "We can stop its hosts so that's going to have to be enough for now."

"Whoa. Hold up. Are you saying we just kill anyone that thing is able to take over?" Becca asked.

She had just admitted to being used by the thing to destroy the transport so McShane understood why Becca was concerned.

"I didn't say that," McShane protested.

"You said. . ." Becca frowned but he stopped her before she could finish.

"I said, we could stop them," McShane corrected her. "That doesn't always mean we'll need lethal force to do it."

The intensity of the alarm klaxons changed in tone, somehow seeming to increase, which McShane wouldn't have thought possible. He looked up at the ceiling.

"That alarm means we've been breached," Becca said. "Wanna tell me what in the hell is going on out there?"

McShane shrugged. "Your guess is as good as mine but what I can tell you is that we need to get moving."

"No argument on that one," Becca agreed. "The faster we're out of here, the better."

****

"Frag it!" Eph shouted. "This isn't my freaking job, guys! I'm a cook!"

"Cool it, Eph," Mike ordered. "We need help and for better or worse, you're it, buddy."

"Yeah, just man up, man," Hammond said.

The three of them were running down the corridor that led to Airlock 4. It was the deepest of the four locks on Pioneer Four, on the station's lowest level.

"We've got breaches all over the station!" Mike told Eph. "And we're almost certainly the closest people to Lock 4."

"That means we've got to seal it," Hammond barked, stating the obvious.

"I get that!" Eph snapped back at him. "But I. . ."

"But you what?" Mike snorted. "Unless you've suddenly grown gills and can breathe under water, Eph, you're just as screwed as everyone else if we don't get the lock closed."

"I don't understand how the frag it got breached to begin with," Hammond complained.

"What the frag does it matter?" Eph asked.

Neither Mike nor Hammond answered him.

The three of them rounded a bend in the corridor and came to a stop at the doorway that led into the section where Airlock 4 was located. Mike moved to access the computer panel next to it.

"Damn it," Mike slammed a clenched fist into the metal of the wall.

"What is it?" Eph's eyes darted from Mike to Hammond and then back again.

"The section on the other side of this door is flooded," Mike explained. "That means we can't go in without suits."

"Frag," Eph heard Hammond say under his breath.

"So what do we do now?" Eph asked.

"God help us," Mike shouted, noticing that there was water leaking out from the edges of the door they were all standing in front of.

"The water's getting in," Hammond said. "That. . . that's not supposed to be possible. How in the hell could this be happening?"

"Something has to have damaged this door," Mike looked at Eph. "Something on the other side of it."

Eph was clueless. He had no idea what Mike was implying but Hammond surely must have because his face went pale.

"No way!" Hammond bellowed. "No fragging way, man!"

"What the hell is happening?" Eph demanded but both Mike and Hammond didn't seem to hear him.

"Damn," Mike said, his voice sullen with a hint of fear. "We've got to get help, get this door reinforced somehow before. . ."

Mike never got to finish his sentence. Something smashed into the other side of the door with enough force to dent the center of it outward towards the three of them. Within the span of a heartbeat, whatever it was hit the door again causing it to give way. The door blew out of its frame, killing Mike instantly as it did, squishing his body against the far wall. Water exploded from the opening into the corridor with enough force to knock both Eph and Hammond from their feet. They went down splashing in its current. Eph caught a glimpse of inhuman, glowing eyes in the water. He only saw them for the briefest of seconds but that was enough to scare the hell out of him. Though Eph had never seen a creature from the depths of the Deep Black in real life, he knew that those eyes had to belong to one of them. And this creature. . . was inside the station!

Eph felt Hammond's hands on him. The next thing he knew, a door was swishing shut, and they weren't caught in the rushing water anymore.

"Wha. . .? How?" Eph stammered.

"I got us into the closest room," Hammond answered but his attention wasn't on Eph. "We're safe."

"Are we?" Eph asked, wide-eyed, looking at Hammond.

"You saw it too then," Hammond's voice was low, little more than a whisper. "Then I'm not crazy."

Eph kept his own voice as calm as he could. "Yeah, I saw it. There's one of those things from the Deep Black out there in the corridor."

"Must have got in through the lock," Hammond said, "But how?"

"I'm a cook, remember?" Eph answered. "How the hell should I know? Besides, we don't even know what happened to the lock or how it was breached, do we?"

Both Eph and Hammond flinched as a horrid noise, like fingernails on a blackboard, came from the other side of the door.

"Frag! It's found us!" Hammond cried out, looking around the room for something, anything to use as a weapon.

Eph turned to look at the door as he backpedaled away from it.

Razor-sharp claws that gleamed in the harsh overhead lights of the room pierced the door where it was sealed on the right side. Metal whined and creaked as scaled hands bent the door back. Much to their surprise, no water came rushing into the room through the opening. Even Eph, though he was far from being an engineer, knew that meant something had been done to Airlock 4 to keep the station from flooding. That was when he realized the alarm klaxons had stopped blaring. Any elation Eph might have felt about not drowning was chased away by the current imminent threat to his life from the creature that had finished tearing through the doorway and now stood only yards away from him. The thing was seven feet tall and covered in gray, thick scales from head to toe. It stood like a man on two legs though its back was slightly hunched. The creature's chest heaved in and out rapidly as if it was relearning how to breathe. And that looked to be exactly what it was doing, though Eph didn't understand how.

The room they were in was a partly filled storage area. Hammond lunged for the closest box, ripping it open in the desperate hope of finding something useful inside. The creature was still adapting to its surroundings but lurched towards Hammond anyway. A loud, angry hiss emerged from its throat as the thing opened its mouth to reveal the dagger-like teeth within it.

"Hey!" Eph yelled, drawing the creature's attention to him. He couldn't just let the thing kill Hammond and between the two of them, at least Hammond had a chance of finding something that could be used against the creature.

Eph's heroism was brief lived. The creature was far faster than it looked. It sprang across the room, lashing out at him. Claws opened up the flesh of Eph's chest, nicking the bones of his ribs, and splattering blood into the air. Eph reeled backwards but there was no escaping the creature's fury. A scaled hand shot out, shoving him the rest of the way towards the wall behind him. Eph was smashed into it. The impact knocked the breath out of his lungs. As he struggled to suck air back into them, the creature gutted him. Its claws opened up his abdomen, spilling his intestines at his feet as Eph howled in pain. He flopped over to the floor as the creature let go of him and turned back towards Hammond.

Hammond had found a crowbar among the crates and boxes stored in the room. He held it, ready to swing, as if it were a baseball bat.

Hammond held his ground, allowing the creature to close in on him. As it did, he swung the crowbar with all his strength. It made contact with the side of the creature's head with a loud thud. The creature lost its balance, lurching sideways, as Hammond struck again. He raised up the crowbar and brought it down with both hands on the creature's back. The creature grunted but didn't fall. It rose up, lashing out to knock the crowbar from Hammond's hands. The makeshift weapon clattered across the store room floor. Hammond's eyes went wide as the creature grabbed him by the throat, tips of its claws sinking into his flesh. Blood spurted out from where they entered. He screamed, thrashing about, trying to get free of the thing's hold. His efforts were in vain though. The creature was a hell of a lot stronger than he was. Its jaw unhinged as the creature's mouth opened impossibly wide. The last thing Hammond saw was the creature's razor-sharp teeth before they bit his face off.

Eph watched Hammond die. With his guts piled up in front of him, there wasn't a thing in hell he could have done to help Hammond. Eph lay in a puddle of his own blood as the creature returned its attention to him. Tears welled up in his eyes and Eph wept openly as he waited for the creature to reach him and his turn to die.

****

Chief Beckett ran for his life. His legs pumped beneath him and his breath came in ragged gasps as he pushed his body to its limits and beyond them. The creature continued to gain on him. The chief could hear its heavy footfalls growing closer and closer behind him. It was hard to believe how everything had gone to crap so quickly. Beckett blamed himself.

He had been on duty in the station's operations room when it all happened. Crazy as it seemed, one second, all lights were green and his mind just drifted off into nothingness. He was calm and at peace. The next second. . . Bam! Beckett snapped back, alert, to see that all of the station's locks were either open or blown. Somebody in the Stomper Bay had to be responsible for it. Beckett hoped that bastard, whoever it was, had drowned when the ocean came crashing into the Stomper bay, flooding it. As soon as he'd woken up, Beckett did all he could to limit the damage and flooding of the station. Getting the locks closed wasn't easy but he'd managed to get two of them resealed and the water coming in from the others cut off by emergency bulkheads. Power was down in several sections and all he could do was hope it stayed on in those that still had it. He hadn't been able to raise anyone over the comms. It was as if some outside force was jamming them. Then his time had run out. A monstrous thing burst into the operations room and there was no choice but to run and that was what Chief Beckett was still doing.

Chief Beckett rounded a corner, his feet slightly sliding on the metal of the floor as he made his turn, but managed to keep his balance. A pair of hands came out of nowhere, grabbing the chief and pulling him out of the way as a heavy assault rifle opened up. It roared in the corridor, a series of deafening booms that echoed off the walls and made Chief Beckett grit his teeth against the pain they bought to his ears. The hands that yanked him aside belonged to a young Stomper pilot, Noah, and the burly man blasting away on full automatic was Sergeant Riggs.

Riggs' burst of fire caught the creature chasing the chief squarely in the center of its gray scaled chest. High velocity, armor piercing rounds ripped through the armor of its scales sending black blood splattering everywhere. The creature screeched and wailed, stumbling, as Sergeant Riggs adjusted his aim, and blew the monster's head into a mess of exploding, gory pulp.

"Frag!" Chief Beckett blurted out as the creature's now headless body toppled to the floor of the corridor.

"Chief!" Noah exclaimed as if just recognizing who he had saved.

Beckett patted Noah on the shoulder as the young pilot released him. "Thanks for the save, Noah. I was sure that thing was going to have me for a late night snack."

"I wouldn't thank us yet, Chief," Riggs snorted.

Chief Beckett shot him a questioning look.

"I'm just glad to see you, Chief," Noah said. "We need all the help we can get."

"How many of those things got in?" Chief Beckett asked.

Riggs shrugged and then shook his head. "Too many."

Chief Beckett gestured at the rifle Riggs was carrying. "You guys raided the armory?"

"Yep," Riggs answered. "Here. You're gonna need this."

Riggs handed him a heavy revolver that had been tucked in his belt.

"So where's everyone else holed up?" Chief Beckett asked.

"There ain't no everyone else, Beckett," Riggs told him. "You're looking at everyone on this station that's still alive right now."

"We don't know that for sure," Noah protested.

"Kid, you seen anyone else that hasn't been halfway eaten or didn't have their limbs torn off?" Riggs said flatly.

Noah didn't say anything. The expression on his face told Chief Beckett how right the sergeant likely was.

"God help us," Chief Beckett muttered. He took a moment to wrap his mind around everything he had just found out and then said, "So, gents, what's the plan?"

"Stay alive," Riggs grunted.

"Were you able to get a distress signal out?" Noah asked Beckett, desperate hope in his eyes.

"No," Chief Beckett frowned. "We're on our own."

"Well, regardless, we can't stay here," Riggs said. "We're sitting ducks out in the open like this."

"Where should we. . . " Noah started to ask but the sound of his voice was drowned out by the screeching cries of a pack of creatures that came tearing around the bend in the corridor at them.

"Holy frag!" Noah shouted, yanking up his rifle, both hands clutching it tightly, as he opened fire. The young pilot sent one of the creatures to hell as Riggs' rifle roared, killing another. The creatures had come upon them too fast. It was too little too late to save them. The other three creatures in the pack were in melee range now. Noah died; a creature removed half his face with a single swipe of its claws.

"Kid!" Riggs yelled as Noah went down but that was all he had time to do. All his attention returned to just trying to save his own butt. The sergeant rammed the tip of his rifle's barrel into the scales covering the stomach of the creature he was engaged with and pulled the trigger. The point blank burst blew a hole clean through the thing's abdomen. Riggs threw himself away from its collapsing corpse, swinging his weapon around, trying to bring it to bear on the next closest of the creatures but its clawed hands snatched the barrel of the rifle, wrenching it away out of his grasp.

Chief Beckett watched in horror as the creature that had disarmed Riggs plunged the claws of its hands into the sergeant's chest. With a violent jerk, the thing tore apart the sergeant's ribcage in an explosion of hot red.

His instincts took over as Chief Beckett's revolver boomed in rapid succession. His first shot blew a chunk of meat from the shoulder of the creature that killed Riggs. The second grazed the side of its neck as the thing tried to dodge the bullets coming at it. The third shot missed entirely. Beckett quickly tried to adjust his aim but the creature plowed into him, taking him backwards into the corridor wall. Beckett heard the sound of his bones breaking inside of his body deep in his ears as the creature's weight smashed into him. Blood spurted from his mouth like vomit. Beckett knew he was dead, his body just hadn't fully realized it yet. With the last of his strength, he pressed his revolver to the side of the snarling monster's head and squeezed the trigger. As Beckett lost consciousness and his life left him, his mind wondered why his ears registered three gunshots, not one.

****

Marshal McShane and Becca had heard the battle from a distance, running in its direction, wondering what in the hell was going on. Neither of them were expecting to come face to face with creatures from the Deep Black. Several of the things lay dead on the corridor floor along with the bodies of Sergeant Riggs and Noah. There were two creatures that were very much alive though. One had Chief Beckett pressed against a wall, pinning him there as one of its clawed hands dug and twisted about inside of him. The other came charging at them, snarling and screeching in a berserk frenzy. McShane fired twice, putting a round into the skull of each monster. Beckett got off a shot at the exact moment too. The creature that was pinning him. . . its head pretty much disintegrated as McShane's shot added to the damage of the chief's. Then it was all over.

Becca started towards Chief Beckett as he slid down the wall, his back smearing red along it, but McShane put out a hand, stopping her.

"Leave him be," McShane said. "He's dead."

McShane gave her a second before adding, "We need to get back to the main lab. I left Dr.

Lowery there. If those creatures are loose in the station. . ."

"I get it!" Becca snapped. "Let's go."

Becca paused long enough to scoop up an assault rifle from the bloody mess on the floor and then led the way. McShane followed after her, allowing Becca to take point. She was a trained soldier who was now armed so he saw no need to protect her.

They reached the main lab without another encounter but McShane knew that was just luck. There had to be more of the things inside the station.

The lab was dark as they entered it. The main lights were off. There was only the dim red glow of the emergency lighting above them. It made everything in the room seem like it was bathed in human blood. McShane didn't see Dr. Lowery. He figured she'd be on them with questions the second they came in. His gaze scanned the room in search of her.

"Oh, sweet heaven," Becca stammered.

McShane turned to look in the direction that she was and saw Dr. Lowery. She hung from one of the lab's walls, impaled there by the metal leg of a lab table that had been plunged through her heart and into the bulkhead.

Dr. Jeffery stepped out of the shadows, the lab's door clanging shut behind him.

"Welcome, Marshal," Dr. Jeffery greeted them with a smile. "I see you've brought a friend."

"Jeffery?" Becca asked. "Is that you?"

McShane couldn't tell if she just hadn't fully recognized him or if she was asking something else entirely.

The thing in the doctor's body clapped its hands slowly in front of it. "You see, don't you, child?"

"That's not Jeffery," McShane confirmed for Becca, aiming his pistol at him.

"No. I'm not," the doctor's eyes burnt red, brighter than the glow of the emergency lights. "I am. . .more. Much more."

"Don't take make another move," McShane warned. "I don't give a damn what you are. I'll end you if you do."

"There's no need for that, Marshal," Jeffery purred. "I've already won and there isn't a thing you can do about it."

"Frag you!" Becca yelled, squeezing the trigger of her rifle.

Bullets shredded the flesh of Jeffery's body, tearing his upper torso apart. He crumpled to the floor and lay there twitching. Becca had emptied her rifle into Jeffery so she rushed to stand over him, bashing the butt of it down into his skull, over and over, until bone gave way, blood and brain matter spilling out.

"Ease up," McShane told her. "He's dead."

As Becca's head turned around towards him, her eyes were burning just as bright and hot as

Jeffery's had been. Her lips parted in a feral smile.

"You see now, don't you, Marshal?" the thing within her asked him. "I've won. It's all already over. Let me into your mind and you'll be free, released just like this woman has."

"Not a chance in Hell," McShane growled as his pistol came up. He put a round between Becca's eyes that blew most of her brains out through the gaping exit hole it made in the back of her skull. She died instantly, leaving him alone in the sealed lab.

His pistol fell from his trembling hand, dropping onto the floor at his feet.

He knew that the thing in Becca hadn't been killed with her. He'd merely loosed it again. McShane could feel its phantasmal essence trying to get inside of him. It wanted him. . . needed him in order to keep reaching out to spread itself further out into the world. It wanted to reach the surface and through him, it could do just that. All of the station's escape pods remained intact.

McShane walked to the closest computer console and was relieved to see that it still had power. His fingers chattered away on the keys of its keyboard inputting his personal authority codes.

In his mind, McShane could hear the monstrous, intangible entity from the Deep Black roar in fury as he finished activating

Pioneer 4's self-destruct sequence and its timer began counting down.

"Frag you," McShane smirked.

Seconds later the entire station exploded as its nuclear core detonated, flashing like an exploding super nova on the ocean floor.

END

AUTHOR BIO

Eric S Brown is the author of numerous book series including the Bigfoot War series, the Psi-Mechs Inc. series, the Kaiju Apocalypse series (with Jason Cordova), the Crypto-Squad series (with Jason Brannon), the Homeworld series (With Tony Faville and Jason Cordova), the Jack Bunny Bam series, and the A Pack of Wolves series. Some of his stand alone books include War of the Worlds plus Blood Guts and Zombies, Casper Alamo (with Jason Brannon), Sasquatch Island, Day of the Sasquatch, Bigfoot, Crashed, World War of the Dead, Last Stand in a Dead Land, Sasquatch Lake, Kaiju Armageddon, Megalodon, Megalodon Apocalypse, Kraken, Alien Battalion, The Last Fleet, and From the Snow They Came to name only a few. His short fiction has been published hundreds of times in the small press in beyond including markets like the Onward Drake and Black Tide Rising anthologies from Baen Books, the Grantville Gazette, the SNAFU Military horror anthology series, and Walmart World magazine. He has done the novelizations for such films as Boggy Creek: The Legend is True (Studio 3 Entertainment) and The Bloody Rage of Bigfoot (Great Lake films). The first book of his Bigfoot War series was adapted into a feature film by Origin Releasing in 2014.

Werewolf Massacre at Hell's Gate was the second of his books to be adapted into film in 2015. Major Japanese publisher, Takeshobo, bought the reprint rights to his Kaiju Apocalypse series (with Jason Cordova) and the mass market, Japanese language version was released in late 2017. Ring of Fire Press has released a collected edition of his Monster Society stories (set in the New York Times Best-selling world of Eric Flint's 1632). In addition to his fiction, Eric also writes an award-winning comic book news column entitled "Comics in a Flash" as well a pop culture column for Altered Reality Magazine. Eric lives in North Carolina with his wife and two children where he continues to write tales of the hungry dead, blazing guns, and the things that lurk in the woods.

Made in the USA
Coppell, TX
22 April 2024

31603948R00079